THE GIRL WITH A SECRET

THE GIRL WITH A SECRET

THE LAST VAMPIRE™ BOOK 3

JUDITH BERENS   MARTHA CARR   MICHAEL ANDERLE

LMBPN Publishing
PMB 196, 2540 South Maryland Pkwy
Las Vegas, NV 89109

First US edition, June 2019
Print ISBN: 978-1-64202-806-5

Thanks to the JIT Team

Jeff Goode
Angel LaVey
Daniel Weigert
Jeff Eaton
Micky Cocker
Dorothy Lloyd
Paul Westman

If we've missed anyone, please let us know!

Editor
SkyHunter Editing Team

DEDICATIONS

From Martha

To everyone who still believes in magic
and all the possibilities that holds.
To all the readers who make this
entire ride so much fun.
And to my son, Louie and so many wonderful friends who
remind me all the time of what
really matters and how wonderful
life can be in any given moment.

From Michael

To Family, Friends and
Those Who Love
To Read.
May We All Enjoy Grace
To Live The Life We Are
Called.

CHAPTER ONE

Vickie's heart seemed to pound almost out of her chest as she sipped on her glass of water at the kitchen table.

Her companions struggled to calm her, and all they could do was soothe her and try to keep her vampire powers contained and hope this sense of panic would pass. She had already destroyed the side door, and they didn't want to risk the very real possibility that she'd lose control and break something else.

"You won't be able to get back to sleep, will you?" Alexis rubbed her eyes.

"I don't know," the vampire muttered and huddled miserably in her chair. "I can't shake this feeling that something awful is brewing. It's somewhere and it's getting closer, but I don't know where, or when, or even why."

Craig scratched the back of his head and released a long, loud yawn. "Is this the worst it's been? Or have you felt this way at school? Maybe it's only something here in the house."

She knew better. "No, I don't feel it at school." *I feel it whenever I'm around Will, but I can't tell you that because I don't want Alexis to feel bad about the guy she's dating.*

"Maybe if you went to bed and read a book for a while." His eyes drooped involuntarily. He used every last ounce of energy in his body to keep himself alert, but it made little difference.

"I don't think that will work."

"It has to be better than you shattering my back door again. I'll have to replace the whole door now."

"I'm really sorry." She hadn't intended to destroy property, especially in her family's own house. But when her instincts kicked in, she was very difficult to control.

"Don't apologize. I'm only giving you a hard time. We'll get to the bottom of it somehow, but for now, you need to get some sleep."

Everyone retired to their bedrooms. As she'd predicted, Vickie sat in bed and stared at the wall, her stomach still twisted in knots. Her legs twitched and bounced.

You need to get your mind off this if you want any chance of falling asleep. She grabbed the new e-reader Craig bought for her and tried to distract her mind with a little fiction.

Alexis had recommended a series about a girl adjusting to a new school in a new town. She'd said it was really well-written and the vampire would see some parallels between herself and the main character.

Vickie enjoyed reading and especially fiction, which wasn't very common back in her day. But that night, no reading was in the cards.

It proved too difficult to concentrate on the story. As

her gaze pored over the words on the screen, images flashed in her mind. With every new image, she startled.

An unrecognizable vampire spun in circles and flailed her arms and legs.

Dark figures draped in black robes circled her to close her in.

The vampire hissed, bared her teeth, and lunged at whichever robed figure was closest to her.

Vickie couldn't recognize any of the figures. The vampire's face was covered by her long, dark hair. But when she saw the fangs, she knew the girl was dealing with a threat to her life.

A little desperate, she shook her head, stepped out of bed, and paced feverishly in her room. She tried to stretch her legs and calm her mind with an endless repeat of mental assurance.

It's not real. Whatever it is, it's not real. You're only imagining things. You probably simply need to get some sleep, that's all.

Any time she tried to settle and read, the images would flash again. They would take split seconds to appear and disappear, but she could see them clearly.

Vickie broke out in a nervous sweat as the images grew more violent. The robed figures shot the girl repeatedly. She sank her fangs into the necks of some of them in retaliation. Blood splattered everywhere to stain her white gown and the concrete below them.

A few of her attackers managed to secure her by the arms, lifted her off the ground, and presented her to one of the other robed figures.

She snapped back to reality, her mind foggy. Each time

the images flashed, she grew more and more concerned that they were real. She knew it was her imagination, but she couldn't help being utterly terrified.

It's not real. Or is it? Is it a vision of something that will happen? Am I only being paranoid? Maybe I simply need sleep. Or maybe I need to be alert? Is this something that is coming?

Another flash broke her train of thought. The man moved closer. In the next snatched image, he drew a knife. The scene snapped into another in which he pressed the blade of the knife against the girl's throat. It flashed again, and the men holding her yanked her by the hair and dragged her head back to expose her neck.

In that last moment frozen before her eyes, Vickie realized the girl in the vision was her. *That's not me. That's only an image of me. It means nothing.* Despite her internal pep talks, she couldn't prevent the images from pushing past her reason. When the man dragged his knife across her throat, she grasped her own neck in agony and tried not to scream. She threw herself back onto her bed and shook her head violently until she finally snapped out of it.

When the vision finally passed, she sat up and looked around in confusion. Her e-reader was gone and she was alone. The metal bed frame was bent in the middle where she had thrown herself down.

Her fingers had ripped holes in the mattress. A hasty glance revealed her e-reader on the other side of her bedroom where it lay peacefully beneath a fresh hole pounded into the drywall.

Vickie sat on the ground, fearful that she would destroy anything or anyone if they crossed paths with her on the wrong day. Her powers were too great—and too damaging.

Alexis knocked on the door and walked in. "What is going on?"

"I…I don't know. I keep seeing things and I'm worried that they will become a reality."

"Like what?"

"Bad things. Things that vampires dread."

She shook her head in an effort to fight the next onslaught. The visions weren't over yet. Another sequence thrust into her awareness while Alexis stood beside her. The vampire could almost feel the hands that grasped her and compelled her to hold still. Even the sharp blade in the vision could be felt—something that scared her more than anything else.

Her dream self caught hold of one of the robed figures and threw him. But in real life, she grabbed the other girl by the shoulders. In one shove, she tossed her sister over the bed and into a painful sprawl on the floor on the far side.

Her innocent victim tried to fight her tears, and Vickie clicked back to reality and ran to her. "Are you okay? I'm so sorry. I didn't want to do that. I don't know what came over me."

Alexis crawled to her feet, clutching her cheek and her arm. "I got a few new injuries today, I guess."

After repeated assurances that she was okay, the vampire told Alexis to go back to bed and she was left alone again. This time, however, she was tired and knew the immediate threat was gone. She crawled under the covers and tried to avoid the new holes she'd poked into the mattress as she drifted off to sleep.

The next morning, Vickie moaned as she walked down the hallway. The air was thick and humid, and she broke out into a sweat simply from walking through the house.

"Why does it feel like I'm wearing a blanket of heat across my shoulders?" she asked. "I can't believe how hot it is."

"Welcome to Wisconsin." Alexis sighed. "We're usually good for one or two unseasonably warm weeks per year. How did you stay cool in Salzburg?"

She scanned her memory for a moment. "We didn't. There weren't any heat waves like this. Ever. At least, not while I was alive." She poured herself a bowl of cereal.

Craig stood and walked down the hall to his room. On his way, he glanced into Vickie's room and saw the new hole in the drywall. *Not again.*

He returned to the kitchen where the girls were still eating. "Vickie, we need to talk." He pulled a chair up to the table and sat. "What happened last night?"

She tried to wave it off. "I...uh, had a bad dream, that's all. It felt so real, I thought I was in the dream. When I woke up, the damage was done."

"You can say that again. Is this something that will get better over time, or will you always be paranoid about people coming after you? I don't want to sound cruel, but I need to know because Alexis and I can't follow you around with a mop and a rag to clean up after you every minute of the day. You have to find a way to get this under control."

"Besides the cleanup," Alexis added, "you'll hurt people. Or yourself."

Vickie nodded. She agreed wholeheartedly, but she also didn't quite understand what was happening either. The truth was that she was as clueless as they were. Still, to soothe their concerns, she agreed to work on it.

After Craig stood and went to his room, her sister leaned in. "Do you really think you'll be able to resolve this?"

"What choice do I have? I can't live like this forever." She shrugged. "But I'll tell you right now, if someone wants me dead, I'll kill them all first." She noticed the other girl move her arm gingerly. "How's your shoulder?"

"It's fine."

That was the part that scared her the most. *If I damage a wall or a piece of property, fine. I can deal with that. But if I lay my hands on the people who trust me the most, I will be kicked out of here, left on the curb somewhere, and I'll have to beg people for money.*

"Why didn't you tell your dad about it?" she asked.

"We don't need you in trouble, Vickie. Not right now, anyway. It was an accident. I'll feel better soon and it's only a bruise. I didn't tell him because I don't want him to send you away. And I believe we can still rein this in. If we do that, it won't be an issue anymore. You've done great so far and we only have to do a little better, that's all."

Not unless I kill you before we find the answers. Please, God, don't let me do that.

As she finished her breakfast, she smiled and stared at the ceiling. The feeling in the pit of her stomach was gone in that moment. *Maybe it was a temporary thing. Maybe it was only a bad dream that got out of hand.*

Either way, she savored feeling comfortable and at

peace again. After such a stressful night, it was a welcome change of pace.

The two of them changed and got ready for school. After they were dropped off, the girls walked up the sidewalk to the door.

Vickie turned to Alexis. "You know, losing control at home is one thing. What happens if I do something like that here?"

"Given the damage you're capable of, I assume you'll wind up getting sued for the costs of fixing everything. Breaking our side door is nothing. I can't imagine how much it would cost if you had to, like, restore a locker room or something. You don't have that kind of money."

"It's not only the property damage I'm worried about." She gritted her teeth. "I've been terrified of being outed at school. What if everyone found out what I am? What if I lose control and slip up in front of other students?"

"Well, you can forget about friends, laughing with your buddies, and overall being seen in public. No one would hang out with you except me." She kicked a small rock lying on the sidewalk. "Then again, friends would be the least of your problems. The school would put you on the federal government's doorstep in a heartbeat, and that's the last place you want to be."

"Why?"

"They will take over your entire life and won't listen to you. They won't treat you like a girl but as a science experiment. You'll become less of a person and instead, they will make you feel like you're a freak. And you're not. Besides, even if you did nearly kill me last night, I would miss you." She nudged her with her elbow and winked at her.

They separated, and Alexis turned to watch her adopted sister walk away.

She still needs your help. In fact, now more than ever. Suck it up. Your shoulder will heal. Help her keep it under control so she doesn't do it again. If she does, next time, you might not be so lucky.

CHAPTER TWO

That weekend, Vickie walked out of her bedroom in her swimsuit with a towel wrapped around her neck. "Why do you have a pool if you never use it?"

Craig laughed. "People who own pools never use them. It's a universal thing. Unless you have people over, you stay inside. They're a lot of work to clean and maintain."

"Then why have it?"

"Because when you want a pool, it's nice to have." *When you say it out loud, that's a really dumb reason to have anything.*

Alexis wandered through with her phone in her hand and swiped it to check her weather app. "It is a steamy ninety-five degrees outside, and Jess and Jamie are on their way over."

"I hope this is fun," the vampire said and stared at the pool through the glass patio door. "I've never gone swimming before."

Craig filled a glass with water and took a sip. "You mentioned that when you got here this summer. So you never dipped in a lake or anything back at home?"

"Only to bathe." She shook her head. "We had no need to swim. The air was never that hot—and certainly not this hot."

"You'll love swimming." Her sister patted her on the shoulder. *Maybe this will relieve some of the stress she's been under. Otherwise, she'll put us both in the hospital and tear this house to pieces.* "It's the perfect day to do it. When it's this hot, the only place to be is in the pool."

"Girls, make sure you hang the pool cover after you crank it up. Make the pool look nice. This is probably the last time you'll use it this year anyway."

"You got it, Dad." Alexis pulled the patio door open and stepped outside with Vickie close behind her.

Craig stared out at the two girls while they put their towels on the patio table and headed to the pool.

Those swimsuits make me nervous, Carol. I don't know how you would handle them. Teenage girls walking around in bikinis? The boys would be all over them. I need to have a shotgun around here to keep everyone in line. He smirked at the thought.

Of course, he already knew whose side Carol would have been on if she had been there. She would always side with Alexis. To her, Vickie would have been no different, either.

She liked to say, "You have no idea what it's like to be a teenage girl." She was right. He didn't have a clue, so when it came to matters like clothes and makeup, he let her make the rules.

Without a mother around to guide her, Alexis ran the risk of going off-course. Her father dreaded it. If she coped with the lack of a mother by chasing boys or getting involved in drugs, he didn't know if he could ever forgive himself.

Whenever he caught himself thinking like that, Carol's voice rang in his ears again, as if she stood right beside him now and watched their little girl take the cover off.

"We did a good job of raising her. You have to trust her."

Outside, the girls stood on opposite sides of the pool while Alexis turned the crank. Slowly, the blue solar cover retreated from the surface of the water and rolled around a pole that spanned the above-ground pool.

"Grab that end, I'll grab this end. The hooks are on the fence over there." With one big hoist, the girls heaved it off and walked it carefully to the fence. Water dripped onto the overgrown grass that flourished with the regular watering it would receive during the summer whenever someone went swimming.

"There." Alexis clapped her hands. "The temperature of the water is, like, eighty degrees, so it'll be nice and warm."

Vickie approached the pool and rested her arms on the edge while she looked into the crystal clear water. "What do you do in here?"

"Splash around, play games, or float. We'll get in there and cool off, mainly. I'll grab us a couple of sodas from the fridge and we can hang out and listen to music."

I hope it's as fun as she says it is because it doesn't sound fun. It sounds boring. We can do so much more in the air-conditioned house. Why waste our time in here?

Alexis returned from the house with a couple of cans of soda. She placed them on the edge. "Ready to go in?"

"I guess so. I don't know what I'll do in there, but I guess so."

"Vickie, do me a favor. Stop thinking so much. Swimming is fun. That's why Jess and Jamie are coming over to do it too. Get in and relax a little, will you?"

The girl slipped a ponytail holder off her wrist, gathered her hair into a ball, and twisted the holder around it to make a sloppy bun. "I usually don't like to get my hair wet, but we'll see."

She climbed the ladder and lowered herself in the water. A smile swept across her face. "Oh, man. I don't think the water has felt this good in years. Get in."

Vickie followed cautiously, and as soon as she was all the way in, she noticed a big difference between walking around in water and walking around the yard. "I feel…light."

"Everyone does." Alexis laughed. "That's because water is denser than air. Remember your science studies? We have buoyancy. So you can do things like this…"

She raised her feet, leaned back, and paddled around while she stared at the sky. This was one of her favorite things to do in the pool. It was the first thing her mom taught her to do in the water. When she floated like this, her mom had her protected. She'd felt safe.

"Now, let's grab our sodas and hop on some rafts."

There were three rafts. One was a large orange innertube, another a long gray lounge-style affair with a headrest and armrests, and the third was a small hammock-style that kept your head and legs above the water, but allowed everything else to float.

Alexis immediately chose the hammock. "This is one of my favorites. I love being on a raft, but I also love being in the water. This gives me the best of both worlds."

Vickie looked at her options. *I don't know how you get on that circle-shaped thing. The gray one kinda looks like a bed or a couch. I suppose I would know how to sit on there.* She pulled her choice to the ladder, climbed up a few steps, and situated herself carefully.

The companions floated peacefully as the sun beat down on them. The vampire couldn't believe how relaxed she was. After the last few days of anxiety, drifting with no real purpose provided a pleasant change of pace.

Maybe Alexis was right. I only need to relax a little more often. Then I could have better control over these panic attacks I've had lately.

"Happy Fall-in-Wisconsin." Jess laughed as the two of them walked into the back yard from the driveway.

"Hey, girls." Alexis waved. "Sodas are inside. Say hi to my dad and come on out here. The water is perfect."

Minutes later, all four girls were in the pool, sipping on sodas. Jamie commandeered the inner tube, while Jess was content to float on her back until she could have a turn on the rafts.

"We should play a game or something," Jamie said.

"Like what?" Alexis opened her eyes to see everyone's reactions.

Jess looked like she was in favor of a game, but Vickie appeared frustrated. *I thought we were in here to relax. Now we have to play a game too? Make your minds up.*

"Chicken?"

"Ooh, chicken! Yeah, let's do it."

The vampire was slow to get off the raft. Alexis knew why.

"Vickie, chicken is a game where you have two teams and they have to ride each other's shoulders. You try to knock each other over, and whoever can be knocked off their partner's shoulders is the loser."

After a moment, she shrugged and agreed to play. She rolled off the raft and into the water, which was extra refreshing now that she had heated up again in the sun.

Jamie slid over to Jess. "We'll take you two on."

"Bring it," Alexis taunted and turned to Vickie. "Are you sure you can handle this?"

"Sure. It's all good fun, right?"

"Right. And please don't drown me. If I am knocked over, let me go."

She nodded and dipped underwater while Alexis slid onto her shoulders. Vickie stood, and they faced off against their friends.

After a little trash-talking, Jess charged at them with Jamie on her shoulders. Jamie and Alexis giggled as they pushed and shoved each other until finally, Alexis lost her balance, fell into the water with a big splash, and took Vickie with her.

The vampire surfaced and looked at her sister long enough to let her own guard down. With a laugh of real glee, Jamie dropped off Jess' shoulders and the two of them dunked an unsuspecting Vickie and held her head under the water.

She flailed for a moment. Jess released her and swam away while Jamie continued the friendly assault.

In a burst of water, Vickie stood and threw the girl three feet above the surface and flipped her in the air before she splashed into the water. The vampire swam to the edge of the pool and gripped it tightly with both hands while she gasped for air.

"Whoa!" Jess' reaction was understandably strong and she hurried over to her friend to make sure she was okay.

Alexis put her arm around Vickie and whispered into her ear. "This is exactly what we've talked about. Your reaction was too much and now, they'll suspect something's up. Don't use your strength like that. They were only horsing around, which is what you do in a pool."

Vickie swam over and apologized to Jamie, who accepted the apology as she hung her head over the side of the pool and spat out a mouthful of water.

"What was that?" the girl asked, still breathing heavily.

"Oh…" The vampire looked at Alexis, who shrugged and shook her head. "I must have had a little too much adrenaline in me, that's all. I didn't try to hurt you. It was a reflex."

While they talked it over, her sister looked at the edge of the pool where Vickie had held on tightly. Her handprints had been pressed into the metal edge. *I'm surprised she didn't break the doggone thing. Holy cow.*

As Vickie swam back to Alexis, Jamie pulled Jess aside. "I have never felt strength like that before. Ever. Unbelievable."

Her friend shook her head. "You were really airborne there for a few seconds. I'm surprised you're not hurt, but I had no idea Vickie had that kind of power."

"And how does she not even look strong? That baffles

me even more. After being thrown like that, you'd think she had big, bulging muscles everywhere. She's not any bigger than we are."

"One thing is for sure, I won't dunk her again. I've seen what can happen."

CHAPTER THREE

In contrast to the swelteringly hot weekend, Vickie shivered at her desk in the always cold Science Hall. The heat had broken outside and temperatures began to drop back to normal again, but the air-conditioning hadn't been turned off yet.

She rubbed her arms to try to get a little blood flowing to them in the hopes that they would warm up.

Her physical science teacher was a man named Mr. Bilitz. Every girl in class thought he was cute for a teacher, as he was younger with a fresh face, a warm smile, and an always-perfect goatee.

He also worked to keep class fun and exciting, and today was one of his favorite days of the year. As the last few kids took their seats and the bell rang, he smiled and greeted his students from the front of the classroom.

"Today, we get to start on what will be a large portion of your final exam for this semester. It seems like that's a long way away, but it's only a couple of months. I want to give you ample time to work on this project, so we will review the details now and you can have as much time as you need to tweak your design and optimize it."

Vickie looked around the room and saw excited faces from about a third of the students seated there. *They seem to already know what he's talking about. What project is this?*

The teacher walked into the closet at the front of the classroom and emerged with a long triangle made out of wood. It was so high, it reached his chest. "At the end of the semester, we will take this out into that hallway. Each of you will bring a completely homemade car and run it down the ramp. We'll see whose car goes the farthest."

Some of the kids chuckled at the challenge as he continued his explanation.

"We'll do this during the last week of school, and whichever day we choose, I usually like to treat everyone to pizza so we can have a good time, eat good food, and learn about *science*." He gave his customary fist-pump for every time he was able to mention the word "science" directly in class.

"I want you to keep in mind all the laws of motion we have discussed. There are very specific components to cars that address these laws and use them to their advantage. Remember all of those as you build. Use whatever components you want to make them. The car that goes the farthest down the hallway will be declared the winner and will receive a special prize from me."

On the other side of the room, Megan Fitz raised her hand. "What kind of prize?"

He gave a devilish smile. "I don't know yet. I'll make sure it's something good, though, that much you don't have to worry about." He pushed a key on his computer to project the rules onto the whiteboard. "No engines, no electricity, and no external power. The only thing you are allowed to use to propel it forward is gravity and this ramp. Design and build your car for maximum momentum. This means paying close attention to weight distribution, drag and friction, and aerodynamics in general."

Another student raised his hand. "Do you have any tips? Like, where to start? Things to use?"

He turned the projector off and stared into space with a small smile. "Um…I don't have any recommendations on what to use. Honestly, this is the…let's see…sixth year I've run this contest. The winners and runners-up have been made out of everything from wood to plastic to glass. Some have been big while others have been really small. It all kinda depends on what you have to work with. It's much more important to pay attention to this stuff"—he tapped the projector—"than what to use. You can use anything if you build it right.

"One thing I will recommend is that you start early. I can always tell which students started a few months ahead and which ones tried to build it the night before or whatever. The faster you can build it, the more time you have to test it and tweak the design. When people create prototypes, they build quickly and then optimize it. Incremental changes will work wonders."

The more he talked about it, the more excited Vickie became. At first, she was intimidated by a class project. But this was a chance for her to work with her hands on something productive.

As a child living in a castle with livestock outside, she was used to doing any number of menial jobs. She took care of animals, mainly, and that was a lot of hard work. One of the reasons she felt she was antsy all the time was that she didn't really do much physical labor like she was accustomed to.

This project was the perfect fit for her.

But, of course, Megan Fitz had her own plans. As her classmates began to think out loud in reaction to the news of the contest and wonder if their ideas would work, Megan raised her arms in the air.

"Megan, do you have a question?"

She flashed a cocky smile. "More of a statement, actually. Bring it on, everyone. I want you all to write today's date down and note that I will comfortably win this contest at the end of the semester."

Mr. Bilitz rolled his eyes. "Thank you, Megan. All right, if there are no more questions, let's get back to today's lesson."

After class, Vickie stood and walked past Megan, who was still packing her books up. They locked gazes as they had done for weeks.

Since the vampire had retaliated against the bully in the cafeteria, the girls largely stayed away from each other. Megan didn't want to be scared of her, but after she'd felt the brute force her opponent had thrown at her, she also wouldn't mess with her physically.

"Why are you so cocky?" Vickie asked her.

Megan laughed. "I have a few secret weapons up my sleeves."

The two girls walked out of the room. "What, have you built a lot of cars? What makes you more qualified to win this contest than anyone else?"

"My brother won the first-ever contest six years ago when he had Mr. Bilitz. He not only won it, he crushed everyone. No one has built a car that has gone farther than his. He set the record and it still stands."

"So?"

"He's an engineer now, so he's only gotten better. And I'll have him help me."

"That's cheating. You can't do that."

"Watch me, Frau Hewitt. I bet my car goes twice as far as yours."

They continued to walk side-by-side and barely hid their disdain for each other. Neither said a word for a minute. Vickie's mind raced. *What if you made it into a bet? Do you think you could build a car that would beat her? Maybe Dad knows what to do. Or Alexis. If we all teamed up on a car, we could build one that would go farther than hers, couldn't we?*

"Why don't we make it an actual bet?"

Megan was impressed. "Ooh…look at you. All right, let's make it a bet. What do you want to bet?"

"Money?"

"I don't have money." The girl shrugged. "None to bet, anyway."

"Oh. Me neither."

"The bet should be humiliation. I've embarrassed you. You've embarrassed me. We're tied now, Vickie. Let's make it something that would be torture for a full day of school. Like…I think the winner gets to do the loser's makeup for the first day of next semester."

Vickie nodded. "How about the whole outfit? The loser also has to wear whatever the winner chooses."

"You are on." They shook hands and Megan laughed.

"Now, I'm really impressed. I have to start shopping around for outfits for you. Be prepared." She turned away to go down a different hallway to her next class.

After she walked away, the vampire's stomach twisted. *Not again. What is this? Why do I feel so worried all the time? It's not Megan, or I would have felt this way while she was standing next to me.*

She stepped to the side of the hallway with her hand on her stomach and took a few deep, deliberate breaths. Other students pushed and shoved their way down the hall. Her senses heightened and allowed her to hear and listen to almost every conversation in the immediate area. Her gaze darted constantly around her and sweat built up on her skin.

Calm down, Vickie. Don't out yourself. Please don't out yourself. Keep things under control.

With one more deep breath, she stumbled into the flow of traffic and walked to her next class. With every determined step she took, some of the tightness relaxed and she could breathe again. *Hey, I didn't snap and break anything this time. Take your wins where you can get them.*

That was the only anxiety attack she endured that day. But it still worried her. She went through this in some form or fashion every day. There seemed to be something out there that was bad news for her but she had no clue at all about what it actually was.

She met up with Alexis at the end of her last class and told her about the bet she made with Megan Fitz.

"Are you serious?" her sister responded in disbelief. "Her brother is an engineer."

"I don't know what that means."

"It means it's his job to know how to build stuff that accounts for the laws of motion and whatever. It means he's way smarter than the rest of us. You'll be humiliated by her."

For her part, the vampire was still confident. With her shoulders pulled back, she looked down her nose at the other girl. "We'll work together. I'm sure you know a thing or two. Maybe we can pull Dad into this."

"Vickie, Dad is a journalist—and an unemployed one at that. He doesn't have any experience in building model cars. And my car was average at best when I had Bilitz as my teacher."

"Are you saying we can't do this together?"

"No, we'll do it. I'm saying you'll lose that bet for sure, and you should be prepared for whatever humiliating option Megan hands to you. Knowing her, it'll be super-embarrassing for you."

They started walking to Vickie's locker and she stared at the floor, deep in thought.

Did I make a huge mistake in taking this bet? Should I back out of it? Or can I find a way to still crush her? I didn't think this through at all.

CHAPTER FOUR

Alexis walked past her dad's bedroom and saw him slam his laptop shut. He leaned back in his chair, ran his fingers through his hair, and cursed quietly.

She knocked on the door. "Dad?"

He spun in surprise and had obviously not expected her to be there. "Oh, hey, sweetie. How's it goin'?"

"Fine…is everything okay in here?"

He did his best to shrug nonchalantly. "Yeah, everything's fine. Just some work stuff, you know?"

She nodded, then walked in and sat on the edge of his bed. Vickie was at cross country practice, so this was the only time of the day when she could talk to her father on her own. Although they hadn't taken advantage of the opportunity much, she could tell this was a time when he needed her to step in and talk him off the ledge.

"Dad, do you remember when Mom was first diagnosed with cancer?"

He frowned and wondered where she was going with that comment. "How could I forget?"

"When you and Mom first found out, you hid it from me."

Her father nodded. "We didn't know how to tell you right away. We only hid it from you because we didn't want to worry you until we had all the information we could find at our disposal. Then, we could explain it to you the right way, you know?"

Alexis pursed her lips. "Right, but what I never told you was that the day you guys came home from the doctor, I knew something was up and you were hiding it from me."

He snickered. "Really?"

"I'm not stupid, Dad." She tilted her head challengingly at him. "I can tell when something's wrong with you. Even now, you're trying to hide it but I can see in your eyes that you're really ticked off about something."

Craig looked at his closed laptop and sighed. "Yeah."

She crossed her legs and leaned back on her hands. "Okay, so what's going on? Mom's not here to talk to, so you can start talking to me about stuff now."

He raised his eyebrows at such a sweet sentiment from his daughter. A lump formed in his throat. *So thoughtful and caring, exactly like your mother. She really did do a good job of raising you.*

"I lost an advertiser today."

"And what does that mean? Like, I know what advertisers do, but what does that mean for you?"

"It means I lost money. With every episode I put out, I get money from my advertisers and rates have actually increased. Now, I'm out some cash that we can really use."

"How much?"

"About one thousand, five hundred dollars a month."

She leaned forward. "That's… Okay, that's a lot of money, but it's not too bad. We won't end up in the poorhouse or anything as you like to say." She winked and tried to tease a smile out of her father.

He gave her a sad smile. "Yeah, but you don't understand. That's almost half our monthly budget out the window. Without that money coming in, we'll have to start choosing between paying bills and eating dinners."

Alexis laughed. "It can't be that bad, Dad. You can go out and find another advertiser."

Craig flipped his laptop open and shook his head while he pulled his inbox up. "My audience numbers aren't strong enough to simply attract advertisers. It took almost three months of convincing to get this guy on board. Even if I could drum up another advertiser, I'll still be stuck without the money for two to three months while I try to find someone else."

"Okay." She clapped to inject a little energy into the conversation. "Let's do this like Mom used to. Start firing off some ideas and come up with solutions. Good, bad, it doesn't matter. Sitting around here feeling sorry for ourselves won't do a thing. What about Mom's money? Can we use some of that?"

She was referring to the two-hundred-and-fifty-thousand-dollar life insurance payout they'd received. Alexis wasn't aware of how much it was, but she knew it was a decent little chunk of change.

Her father shook his head glumly. "That's all secured. Your mom and I talked about that before she passed. Her wishes were for us to use that to pay off the mortgage on the house so that we'd always have a roof over our heads, then put the rest of it in a savings account for you to go to college. That's where it is."

"And we can't use any of that money?" He shook his head. "Well…that's really nice to have there."

He smiled. "That was the point."

Alexis stared at the floor for a minute and ran some scenarios in her head. She really wanted to help him find a viable solution. "Why did the advertiser pull out?"

Craig sighed. "The last two episodes of *The Truth About...* didn't do so well. Listener numbers were way down from where they were supposed to be. I expected them to grow and I sold him on that idea. But instead of growing, they dipped. He didn't like that, and he pulled the ads."

The Truth About... had done well, but his most recent guests apparently weren't as interesting as he'd assumed. The last guest, a cancer survivor who claimed to have healed her cancer naturally through diet and exercise, attracted strongly negative feedback from listeners who felt she was a liar or a quack at best.

Several doctors who listened to the podcast emailed him to tell him they refused to give those types of cancer patients a platform because of the dangerous information they peddled.

He had thought it was harmless at worst and really interesting at best. Unfortunately, he was wrong.

To her frustration, Alexis couldn't think of another way to help her father. She knew very little about money and even less about podcasting than he did.

"I'll tell you what, Dad. I'll keep thinking of ideas."

"I know you will." He smiled at her and patted her on the knee.

She stood and threw her arms around his neck. "If there's one thing I know about you, Dad, it's that you're a fighter. Don't let this get you down. You'll figure it out. I promise." She kissed him on the cheek and walked out of the room.

Craig closed his eyes for a moment. *How do you get out of this? How do you provide for your family? Why did you take on another mouth to feed when you aren't even able to feed your-self and your own daughter?*

He tried whatever he could to not mope around the house in grief. But parenting alone had taken a toll on him, both mentally and emotionally.

Of its own accord, his gaze drifted to his nightstand, where a short stack of books—all with variations on the title, *How to Raise a Teenager By Yourself*—sat waiting to be read.

Being a widower is tough on its own. Raising a teenage girl is tough on its own. Being a present and attentive parent is tough on its own. Being a provider for your family is tough on its own.

But to have to do all of that at once? It feels impossible.

Consciously, Craig knew it wasn't impossible. He knew he would find his way through it because he had no other choice. There was no way he would ever do anything drastic to hurt himself or Alexis, and the problems wouldn't go away on their own.

So, exactly like his wife used to do whenever faced with an impossible challenge, he would eventually have to push forward and entertain every solution he could think of.

But in order to do that, his emotions would need to be under control, and they weren't.

He followed a blog called Suddenly Single Dad, where a man discussed the challenges and triumphs of raising his two kids after his wife had unexpectedly passed away. The author handled the issues with light humor and considerable empathy, which made him feel a little less alone whenever he read it.

One theme that the author always came back to was "giving yourself a break." Craig had saved an excerpt of a post in his digital notebook so he could always remind himself in darker moments:

It's okay.

It's okay to feel sad.

It's okay to feel overwhelmed.

It's okay to feel like your problems will never be solved.

It's okay to feel alone.

It's okay to feel trapped.

It's okay to feel.

It's okay to not be okay.

When you find yourself buried under these emotions, gasping for air, kicking and screaming to somehow find your way out... tell yourself that it's okay.

Nothing will be solved while you are in the thick of panic and fear.

So let yourself go through it. Let it wash over you.

Feel your feelings. Go down to the depths with them. This, too, shall pass.

Sometimes, you can't force it to pass. All you can do is weather the storm and wait for it to pass on its own.

But keep telling yourself it's okay.

He sat there in his chair and repeated the words, *It's okay,* in his head over and over again. A tear ran down his cheek.

The problems suffocated him with no clear path out.

He wouldn't move to get a new job. There were no more jobs for him in Milwaukee, but he wanted to be near familiar things, especially for Alexis.

All he had was this podcast. It was his best chance to provide for his family.

He smiled and brushed the tear away when he thought about how Carol handled getting cancer.

The first night after the diagnosis, after Alexis had gone to bed, she sat at the kitchen table with her laptop and a notebook and pen and furiously scribbled notes.

She Googled every possible solution, every treatment option, and every chance at survival that she could get her hands on and wrote all of them down.

Some were traditional treatments, like chemotherapy and surgery. Others were a little off the beaten path, like essential oils and dietary restrictions. She noted the details of each one, the known success rates, how difficult it would be to implement them, and whether or not she felt they would be successful.

When she was done, after several hours of notetaking, she had pages and pages full of ideas—both good and bad.

Craig asked her later why she spent so much time writing down the ones she knew wouldn't work.

Carol replied, "Sweetheart, you can't get to the good ideas without going through the bad ones. Get them all on paper first, then you can start picking out the good ones. If you only write down the good ideas, you'll never find the right ideas."

She was so smart. She always knew what to say, when to say it, and how to say it.

Of course, he wished that somewhere in all those notebook pages, she had found the right solution. But there was none.

Looking back on it, he admired her efforts. To the very end, she never gave up trying anything—*anything*—that held the potential to help. To Carol, there were no stupid answers.

If she were here, she would have already jotted down a dozen ideas for me to try. Three or four of them would be usable. She always knew how to find the right answer in a pile of wrong answers. If only she'd been able to find the solution to her cancer diagnosis. This family still needs her.

In that moment, the weight lifted ever so slightly off his shoulders. He scrabbled in the drawer of his desk and retrieved out an old paper notebook.

With his pen in hand, he typed **how to make money with podcasts** in a search box and began to take as many notes as he could cram onto the page.

All right, Carol, help me out here. We have a problem to solve.

CHAPTER FIVE

Craig and the girls wandered the aisles at a pharmacy down the road from their house. It wasn't in the nicest of neighborhoods, but it was the closest place to have a prescription filled, so they used it out of convenience.

"How long will this take?" Vickie asked while they walked up the seasonal aisle, which was already packed with Christmas decorations to Alexis' delight.

"Probably ten or fifteen more minutes," the other girl replied as she picked up a dancing snowman display and pushed the button. It sang "Winter Wonderland" while it shook its hips. She giggled.

"You and your Christmas," her father muttered with a smile on his face. *I guess she could be into worse stuff.*

"How often do you have to do this?" Vickie wasn't being impatient but she simply didn't understand the concept of medication yet.

"Once a month." Alexis replaced the dancing snowman. "If I don't get this stuff, my skin breaks out into so much acne. I get scars on my face, bumps everywhere, and the whole thing turns red. It's really embarrassing."

"Why is it embarrassing?" The vampire frowned as she tried and failed to see the logic of this. "You don't choose to have blemishes on your face. It seems weird to be embarrassed by something that is not your fault."

Craig laughed. "Yeah, well, welcome to being a teenager. It doesn't matter if it's your choice or not. If you look less than perfect, someone will be waiting to make fun of you."

"Dad, we are so coming back here in a month or two to stock up on this stuff." Alexis held up a wreath wrapped in Christmas lights and sparkly garlands.

"Honey, do you have to pick the loudest, most obnoxious decorations in the store? What is it with you and ugly Christmas stuff?"

She placed her hand on her chest and feigned offense. "Dad! There is no such thing as ugly Christmas decorations."

He picked up a mini disco ball wearing a Santa hat. "Really? What is this? It doesn't even make sense."

"It's wearing a Santa hat, Dad." His daughter shrugged. "That makes it a Christmas disco ball. What's there to figure out?"

"Who actually buys this stuff?"

Vickie stared at the dozens of rolls of Christmas wrapping paper that protruded vertically from a box on the shelf. "When you need decorations for this holiday, you come here to buy them? Is this the only store that sells Christmas things?"

Alexis laughed. "No way. Almost every store sells

Christmas stuff. It starts coming out at this time of year, mainly because the world loves me and wants to see me happy in October." She held up a small singing stuffed dog with reindeer antlers and riding on a sled. She pushed the button and it sang "Jingle Bells." On the last chorus, the dog wagged its tail and rang another bell.

Craig recognized the look on his daughter's face. He sighed loudly. "How much?"

"Only $6.95!"

He rolled his eyes. "Fine. We shouldn't even look at this yet," he complained. "The Halloween stuff is one aisle over. We should be getting ready for that."

"What's Halloween?" The vampire wandered to the end of the aisle and turned the corner to see for herself.

"Halloween is actually a great time for you." Alexis beamed with excitement. "I love the holiday season. Halloween is where you decorate with spooky stuff like monsters and goblins and…well, vampires."

"Yeah, this should be right up your alley, Vickie." Craig put a hand on her shoulder and pointed to a Dracula statue. He pushed the button on its base and the eyes lit up with red lights. In an exaggerated accent, it shouted, "I vant to suck your blawwwd!"

Vickie scrunched her face, unimpressed. "This is spooky? These Hollywood vampires are so lame."

"Will we simply dress you up as a vampire, then?" Alexis giggled. "We could save on a little makeup if we do."

"Why do I have to dress up?"

"On the last weekend of the month, someone will wind up having a Halloween party. We'll go, but you have to pick a costume. I think dressing you as a vampire would work really well, actually."

Her sister squinted at her. "I'm already dressed like a vampire. I don't get it."

Craig laughed and pulled a makeup kit off the rack. On the front was a photo of a model with pale makeup and dark circles around her eyes, black lipstick, and large fake fangs. Her fingers were extended like claws as she posed for the camera. "She means dressing you up like a vampire."

She winced. "Maybe. Let's leave it at that for now."

They continued to wander down the aisle and pointed out the big plastic skeletons and glow-in-the-dark witches' masks. "Halloween is the official start of the holiday season," Alexis explained. "It's a stretch of a few months where everything has decorations on it, and each month, there's something fun to celebrate. Halloween in October, Thanksgiving in November, Christmas in December, and New Year's in January. This part of the year jazzes me up."

"Especially Christmas." Craig put his arm around his daughter.

She beamed. "*Especially* Christmas. What's not to like? You give presents out, the music is awesome, decorations are everywhere, the movies are perfect...it's the happiest time of the year."

Craig was happy to hear her say that. *I was a little worried that her mom being gone would dampen her Christmas spirit. It sounds like I won't have to worry about that this year. That's one less thing on my mind, anyway.*

"Alexis Watson, pick-up at the pharmacy window. Your

prescription is ready. Alexis Watson, your prescription is ready."

She pointed to the speaker in the ceiling. "That's me. Let's go get the stuff."

They took a shortcut through a snacks aisle overloaded with chips, popcorn, and candy. "I can't believe how many different things are sold in this one little store," Vickie observed. "It's impressive. If you could only come to one store, you could choose this one and have all your needs covered."

Alexis picked up her prescription and the three of them moved to the line at the register in front of the store. "We still have to pay for my Christmas puppy."

There were two people ahead of them in line, so they waited patiently while the other customers finished paying for their items.

A tall man in dark sunglasses and a baseball hat stood in front of them, next in line. Craig squinted as he watched his body language, then carefully and quietly tugged on both girls' arms to make them back away a little.

His intuition proved to be correct, as the man drew a handgun and aimed it at the cashier, who froze.

"Open the register and no one gets hurt," he ordered. Slowly, she pushed the button to open her register. With his weapon still brandished threateningly, he reached in with his free hand to gather as much cash as he could and shove it into his pockets.

Craig kept one hand on his daughter's shoulder. She trembled with fear while the large man waved his gun around.

Vickie was shaking, too, but not with fear. Rage

bubbled up inside her. He glanced at her as she bared her teeth, her fangs fully extended. She took one step forward but he caught her arm and held her back.

"No," he whispered. "Stay back. This isn't your time to fight."

Once he'd emptied the register, the man sprinted out the front door to an old car that waited out front. He scrambled into the passenger side and it drove off before he even slammed the door shut.

Everyone exhaled. The store manager sprinted to the front to check on everyone.

"I've already pushed the emergency call button. Is everyone okay up here?" He looked in the cashier's eyes and assured her that she'd handled it perfectly. Then, he turned to the girls and their father. "If you're paying with a debit card, I can go ahead and push you through. But you'll probably need to wait so the police can get a statement from you as a witness."

"Are you girls okay?" Craig studied his girls while Alexis placed the stuffed dog onto the counter, her hands still shaking. Both nodded silently.

The manager smiled at Vickie. "Those are great, by the way. If you don't mind me saying."

"What?"

"Your fangs. They look almost real from here."

Her companions shot each other a concerned glance, then looked at the vampire. Sure enough, her fangs were completely exposed as before, ready to attack. She stammered and stuttered as she tried to come up with an explanation while Craig swiped his debit card.

"She has a special pair. They cost a fortune," he said to the manager, who smiled in response.

By the time they had completed the payment, the police had arrived and pulled them aside to have them describe what happened. Craig noted what he could remember about the criminal and what he did.

"Can you remember what he looked like?" The officer flipped a pocket notebook open.

"I can," the vampire said. "He was about five-foot-ten, maybe a hundred and eighty pounds. He wore dark black jeans which were about two sizes too big for his frame. The cuffs were rolled up. He wore white sneakers with a black t-shirt and a navy-blue sweatshirt. He hid behind large dark sunglasses and a New York Yankees baseball cap. After the robbery, he ran out to a running Dodge Neon with purple paint chipped away above and below the gas tank. The license plate number was XHJ-263."

The officer's jaw dropped. He couldn't take the details down fast enough. "That's a heck of an eye you have," he said finally. "Thank you very much, I appreciate it. You folks can go now. Thank you for the help. We should have no problem tracking him down with that to work from."

The cashier and the manager, both speechless and with wide eyes, stared at Vickie as the family walked out the door.

Once they reached Craig's SUV and closed the doors, everyone exhaled.

"This was a good example of the good and the bad of your powers, Vickie," he said. "You were a fantastic help to those police officers in there. Obviously, your super-senses kicked in the second you knew we were in danger."

"Yeah, that part comes pretty naturally to me."

"Which is great, except if it wasn't around Halloween, your fangs would have been a dead giveaway. We need to try to find a way to balance the two or one of these days, someone will know that you're not what you seem to be."

"And if that happens," Alexis said, "you might be taken from us."

CHAPTER SIX

"Are you excited for your first pep rally?" Craig smiled as the girls packed their backpacks at the kitchen table before Jess' sister picked them up.

"I don't know." Vickie shrugged her shoulders. "I'm not even sure what a pep rally is, but I didn't want to ask anyone there and feel weird. Coach Lueck only told me to wear my windbreaker and warmup pants, and we'll get together beforehand."

Alexis zipped her backpack. "You're supposed to wear your uniform if you're on a sports team for the school. But since the cross country uniform is a tank top and a pair of short-shorts, you have to wear that instead. It's all about team pride, school pride, that sort of thing." She walked over to the patio door, cracked it open, and stuck her hand out to check the weather. "Brrr. That heat wave is definitely over."

Her father looked out the bay window at the gray, rainy day in front of them. "We'll probably cover the pool on

Sunday if you two aren't still recovering from dancing the night away."

Alexis straightened the white bandana that covered the top of her head. Braided pigtails dangled out each side. At Clear Lake High School, the pep rally was held during the last two hours of the day. Students got off school, herded into the auditorium, and everyone cheered each other on in the name of team spirit and school pride.

As part of that, they were encouraged to dress in the school colors. Because the colors were red, white, and blue, each class could choose a different one. The freshmen wore red, the sophomores wore white, the juniors wore blue, and the seniors decked themselves out in all three.

"It makes for an interesting-looking hallway when everyone is trying to get to class," Alexis joked as she pulled her jacket on.

"What should I expect?" Vickie asked. "Do I have to do anything?"

The other girl snagged an apple for the road and took a bite out of it. "Yeah, you'll walk out and line up with your team. Coach Lueck will do a little intro, then call your names out one by one. But here's the important part. When they call your name, turn around and face us. You want to face your class. Look for the white."

"And do what?"

"Smile, wave, whatever. Just acknowledge us. Trust me, you'll get cheered."

She was still confused. "I'm not very popular. Why would our class cheer me? Most people don't even know me and half the people who do don't like me."

Her sister closed her eyes and nodded. "Trust me on this one."

"Before you go," her father said, "Vickie, pep rallies are loud. Really loud."

"Definitely." Alexis nodded.

"I don't know how you can do this but find a way to keep your powers under control. Don't let your instincts get the better of you. It's loud but not in a threatening way. So please be careful. Keep your fangs tucked away and don't touch anything or squeeze anything. Remind yourself as often as you have to that this is not a threat. They're cheering for you. It's a fun thing."

Vickie nodded cautiously. *I guess we'll see what happens when I get there. I hope I don't react violently.*

The girls walked out the door to their carpool. He took a deep breath. *I really hope she can learn to not react to everything all the time.*

At the end of the day, the vampire crowded in the hallway with the other Varsity cross country runners. Krista greeted her with an excited smile. "Are you ready?"

"I think so."

"Pep rallies are fun. Like, they're mainly for the football team since they have a game this weekend and no one cares about cross country meets, but we still get a little recognition, which is really nice."

Another girl agreed. "It's like the only ten minutes out of the year that the school remembers they have a cross country team."

The pep rally was underway in the school gym. The hallways rumbled as if a thunderstorm was passing through. Students cheered wildly, stomped their feet on the bleachers, and chanted. Everyone was having a good time.

Vickie held her breath as Coach Lueck announced that they were next. He jogged out to the middle of the gym floor, grabbed the microphone, and gave a short introduction to the cross country team.

He started with the girls' team. "Come on, girls!" Shannon shouted and led them into the gym to thunderous applause.

Vickie's ears rang with the sheer volume of sound coming from her fellow students. They reached the middle of the gym floor and lined up facing their coach. He said a few more nice things about the team, then began introducing them.

Soon, Vickie was up next. *Face your class. Face your class. Face your class.* The sophomore class, decked out in all white, stood on the bleachers in the section behind her.

"And our newest runner, one of the breakout stars of this season, Miss Vickie Hewitt!"

Vickie turned to face the sophomore class, but before she even saw them, the class erupted in cheers so loud, she thought she would fall over. She made eye contact with Alexis, who waved at her and mouthed "wave" to remind her of what to do.

Amidst the cheers, she raised her hand, waved, and smiled from ear to ear at the support from her fellow classmates. Then she stepped back into line.

She remembered little of the rest of Coach Lueck's speech and followed her team out the door when it was time to go. She still wore a somewhat spooked look on her face, which Krista noticed.

"Are you okay over there?" she asked her as they reached the hallway.

"Those cheers. It felt so good."

"Oh yeah, well, you're a sophomore. The thing about pep rallies is the classes all look out for each other. Even if everyone hated you, they'd cheer their faces off for you because you were in their class. It's all a competition to see who can support their class the loudest."

That wasn't the only reason she was full of adrenaline, though. For the first time, she'd been confronted with a loud atmosphere with sudden noises and unfamiliar surroundings and her fangs remained retracted. It was a welcome relief for a girl who struggled to stay hidden.

Once the pep rally was over, students milled around in the halls, still bursting with teenage energy. They high-fived each other, chuckled at their face paint and colorful outfits, and reminisced about the events of the day.

Alexis found Vickie and embraced her in a tight hug. "How great was that? You looked good up there—almost like you belonged."

"Well, that's good, because I felt like I was ready to run out of the gym screaming."

She patted her on the back. "Hey, and the fact that you didn't means you're getting better at this stuff. That's awesome."

The next afternoon would be the start of a long weekend for the girls, and not only because they were headed to the Homecoming Dance. As was tradition, they would meet up with their dates to watch the game together.

That meant Will Rasch and Vickie would need to be near each other with no possibility of escape.

Before they walked out the door to the car, Vickie stopped in the bathroom to give herself a pep talk in the mirror—quietly enough that no one could hear her.

"You need to do this. Do it for Alexis. She likes this guy. You don't have to be friends with him. Just ignore your instincts. And look on the bright side. You'll be there with Eric, who you are crazy about. This is supposed to be a fun thing. Let it be fun."

When they arrived at the game, the two boys greeted them with smiles and bags of popcorn.

But when Vickie and Will saw each other, their smiles instantly vanished. He seemed incapable of smiling at her, and she tried to shake off the feeling of dread that filled her when she was around him.

For the entire football game, they sat on opposite ends of the group with Eric and Alexis between them. The game was fun and as boisterous as the pep rally, and the Clear Lake student body showed up in large numbers to cheer their home team on against the rival Central High.

Although she was relatively nervous and on edge for most of the game due to the atmosphere and the presence of someone who claimed to be her mortal enemy, nothing forced Vickie's nerves through the roof like the third quarter of the game.

Clear Lake had taken a commanding lead by three touchdowns, so the energy in the crowd began to calm into excited confidence. The students sat, and Eric glanced at her and took her hand.

They exchanged nervous smiles and both hoped the

other didn't notice how shaky they were or how much sweat was on their palms.

It was the first taste of romance that the vampire had ever experienced in her life, and it rippled through her like lightning.

Her joy was short-lived, though, when she glanced over and saw Alexis and Will holding hands as well. *Why can't I be happier for her? And why does he have to be the one trying to date her? Can't a good guy show her some attention? What'll happen when we all have to hang out? Will and I might kill each other.*

At the end of the game, they released each other's hands and the crowd stood to cheer their team one more time before they headed to the parking lot.

"That was fun," Alexis commented as the group walked together. "Much more fun than when they lost last year."

"No kidding," Eric replied. "Hey, we should double-check plans for tonight." He looked at Will. "You and I will meet the girls at their house at 5:30, right? Then we can make the restaurant by 6:00."

Will said nothing and merely nodded in response.

"Great. We can't wait." Alexis smiled at both of them. Vickie smiled too, then exchanged another concerned glance with Will before they walked to the lot to look for the SUV.

"I'm a little nervous about tonight," she admitted.

"It'll be great." Alexis nudged her with her elbow. "We'll all have fun together. Come on, it's a double date."

"I know… I just get a feeling about Will."

She stopped walking. "Yeah, I noticed that. You two couldn't stop staring daggers at each other during the whole game. Please do me a favor and try to get along tonight. I'm begging you."

Don't ruin her night. Be civil. She doesn't deserve to have her Homecoming ruined. "I'll do my best. As long as he behaves, I'll behave too. I promise."

CHAPTER SEVEN

Vickie looked at herself in the full-length mirror on the back of her bedroom door. Alexis had spent almost an hour curling her hair for her, shoved as many clips in as she could, and sprayed it with hair spray that burned her nostrils.

She adjusted the spaghetti straps on her dress and allowed the rest to flow to the floor. The dark-purple fabric helped highlight the matching shade of eye makeup her sister had chosen for her. The sparkles on the dress shimmered every time she moved.

Her mind drifted back to the days back home, when grand balls were an event for the wealthy in the village. She had never attended one, and neither had her parents. But she knew of others who went. She saw them ride through from time to time in their best finery.

If they could see me now, they would wish they could look this fancy.

When she walked out, Craig was clearing space on his camera. He looked up and smiled at her.

"I know we haven't known each other for very long yet, but I think you look so grown up right now." He laughed. "You look great."

She blushed. "Thanks. Is Alexis ready yet?"

"I haven't seen her."

They heard the doorknob click and Alexis emerged in a baby-blue dress that billowed to the floor. Craig watched her walk slowly down the hallway and a lump formed in his throat. *I can't believe how much that girl looks like her mother. If only she could see how beautiful she is right now.*

"You look great." He choked over the words. His daughter smiled and gave him a hug.

"Oh, man, you look awesome," she almost shouted at Vickie. "Eric will seriously go nuts. How do you feel?"

The vampire clasped the sides of her dress and twirled dramatically. "I feel very fancy, actually."

"You should. You are fancy." The girls laughed and hugged one another carefully so as to not disturb anything.

Craig held the camera up. "All right, ladies, give me a smile." They spun to face him and put their arms around each other as he snapped a picture. "Perfect."

He looked at his daughter's smile in the photo. *I haven't seen her so happy in so long. She'll have a great time tonight. No one deserves it more than her.*

Ten minutes later, the living room was full of visitors. Their partners had both arrived. Eric's parents were with him but Will came alone with no parents.

A car dropped him off but accelerated away before anyone could see who was driving. "Don't your parents want to come in and take pictures, Will?" Craig asked, a little confused by this unusual behavior.

"No, thank you." He walked past him and into the living room.

"I hope I'm doing this right," Craig joked to the other parents as he snapped pictures. "This is the kind of thing Alexis' mom would want to do."

Eric's mom shared a chuckle with him. "As long as everyone's in the frame, I think you're fine. You're doing great."

First, the boys slipped the wrist corsages onto the girls' hands, then the girls pinned the lapel corsages onto the boys' jackets. Everyone paused to smile for pictures throughout the process.

"All right, time for the garters," Eric's mom yelled with a smile.

The girls hiked their skirts up for a picture with the garters on their legs. Even though he knew it was coming, Craig still squirmed as he took the picture. *This is where I start getting uncomfortable.*

Each girl then sat while the boys slipped the garters off their legs, and the girls then slid them onto their arms.

It might have been tradition, but Craig didn't care for it. Eric's parents enjoyed it and made sure to take innumerable pictures.

When they had finished with all the typical photos, the kids huddled and talked while Eric's parents embraced. "Our boy is really growing up, isn't he?"

And so is my girl. Craig kept to himself with his hands in his pockets as he quietly observed the scene in front of him. *Carol, if nothing else, I wish you were here so I could have someone to talk to. This is kinda brutal. But you should see our little girl right now.*

"Okay," he announced, "is everyone ready to go?"

Eric's parents rushed over to give their son a hug and tell him to have a good time. They complimented the other members of the party, especially Vickie, for how nice they looked, waved goodbye, and left the house.

"Your chariot awaits." He led them out to the driveway where the SUV was parked. Everyone piled in—the girls far more demurely than usual—and he backed out of the driveway and turned down the road to take them to the restaurant.

Several times during the drive, Craig almost rear-ended other vehicles along the way. He was too distracted by watching the group in the rear-view mirror. *I don't know anything about this Will boy. I don't know where he comes from, what his story is, and what interest he has in my daughter. I trust him about as far as I can throw him.*

In the car, however, there was nothing to worry about. The kids all stared at their phones, took selfies, and made funny faces…except Will, who kept to himself.

"Say you're on the dance floor and you run into Megan Fitz." Alexis laughed. "What do you do?"

Vickie shook her head. "I bet if I give her one look, she'll run in the other direction."

Everyone laughed except Will, who stared out the window.

Craig watched the boy closely. *What is up with him? Why is he here if he doesn't want to have fun with the other kids?*

"So you'll meet your friends at the restaurant, right?" he asked in an effort to keep his mind off the unsettled feeling Will had stirred in him.

"Yeah, Jess and Jamie will be waiting for us there. It's kinda like they're going as each other's dates." Alexis laughed.

Craig cringed as he listened to the conversations the kids had throughout the ride.

"Did Mr. Pringle come to your class to give a speech about 'appropriate dancing' this year?"

"Oh! When he talked about no 'belly-to-butt' dancing, I almost died. I couldn't believe he said that in front of the whole class."

"Who do you think will be chaperoning?"

"I hope not Mr. Gilbert."

"Can you imagine Mr. Gilbert at a dance?"

It was all typical high school chatter. Craig didn't miss high school one bit. Part of him cringed at having to endure the conversation, and the other part cringed because he knew he had two and a half more years of this to listen to—or, at least, until the kids could drive themselves.

But then, if they can drive themselves, that opens up a whole new set of problems. I am seriously not cut out to do this on my own. Carol could handle this so much better than me. She could talk me out of freaking out. I could use a talk right now. Anything other than listening to this nonsense.

He changed the radio to an oldies station. Van Halen's "Panama" rocked. He tapped his fingers on the steering wheel and mouthed the words to himself as they bounced along.

"Dad! Can't we turn on something a little more current? This stuff is ancient. No one listens to this anymore."

"Hey, this is Van Halen, have a little respect. Besides, you will all get to listen to your own music for four straight hours tonight. This is my time."

"Ugh, it's terrible, though."

"When you have your license, you can change the radio station to whatever you want. But until then, I'm the boss."

She rolled her eyes at her father and resumed her conversation.

"Will we go to any afterparties tonight?" she asked the group.

Eric nodded. "I think Brad Kook is throwing a party afterward. I'll meet up with him tonight and see what they say. Maybe we can hitch a ride to Muskego and go to that."

"Uh, Eric?" Craig interrupted. "There will be parents at this party, right?"

"I think so, sir. I don't know, though. I won't know anything until I see Brad tonight."

"If I find out you went to a party after the dance with no parents in attendance, this will be the last time you see either of these girls outside of class. Do you hear me?"

Eric's smile fell.

Craig laughed mentally, satisfied with the threat. *If nothing else, I can still put the fear of God into a high school boy. That has to count for something.*

Of course, he knew that wasn't much of a challenge. He had known the boy for a long time now because he was a good friend of Alexis. Eric was a good kid, and he played by the rules. He knew if he laid down the law to him, the boy would follow. *Put a little guilt into him, and he won't cross me. I almost trust him more than I trust Alexis.*

That wasn't an insult to his daughter, either. She had never been on a real date before. He worried that she might be swept up in the fun of dating and forget about keeping herself safe.

And the vibe he got from Will held little promise. If he could only pin it down to something concrete, he'd feel more in control.

Still, there wasn't much he could do about something that was only an uncomfortable feeling. He pulled the SUV in front of the restaurant, which was two blocks away from the school, got out, and opened the back doors for the kids to disembark.

The girls stopped beside their father while the boys walked in.

"Girls, please have a good time tonight. Vickie, keep everything in check. This is a fun night. Go out there and dance, have fun, and forget about any danger or threats or anything like that. There's no evil out there with you tonight. And Alexis? The boys are evil. Stay away from them." He winked at her.

"Dad—"

"I'm kidding. Look, have fun and please be safe. Behave. Your mother always said that we raised you right. Please don't prove her wrong."

She smiled and nodded. "Don't worry, Dad. She was right. And I'll make sure she stays that way."

They turned and walked into the restaurant while he leaned up against the side of the vehicle with his hands in his pockets.

How quickly life changes. It feels like yesterday that I held you in my arms with your mother's head on my shoulder. Now,

I'm letting you go out on your own and going home to an empty house.

He looked at the sky and thought about his wife once again. With a heavy sigh, he climbed into the SUV to head home.

CHAPTER EIGHT

The group sat at a long table in the middle of the dining area of The Chancery. Decked out in their suits and long, flowing dresses, they stood out against the backdrop of small families out for a casual Saturday night dinner.

Each girl sat across the table from their respective dates, with Alexis in the middle, gazing into Will's chestnut eyes. "Did you grow up around here, Will?"

"Um, no. I grew up in a small town far from here."

"Yeah? Where?"

"You wouldn't know it."

The short answers totally frustrated her as she really wanted to get to know her date a little better. She pressed on. "What do your parents do?"

"My mother stays home. My father works in agriculture." He punctuated every answer with a long beat of silence, his face as expressionless as his tone.

What a fun date. This guy doesn't even have a bad person-

ality—he has no personality. Geez, my first date and he's less than a bump on a log. How can someone so cute be so boring?

For their part, Eric and Vickie had a great time and laughed and joked with each other on her left. On her right, Jess and Jamie chuckled together as usual.

The food arrived at the table. When he saw his plate of spaghetti with meat sauce, Eric pressed his lips together. "Whoops."

Vickie leaned over to look at his plate. "What? Did they get something wrong?"

"No, it's not that, only…" He didn't want to admit his mistake.

"What? What happened?"

"It was stupid of me to order spaghetti."

"Why?"

"I'm wearing a white shirt. This sauce will get all over it and I'll look like an idiot." The group laughed in response and tried to offer their encouragement. "I suppose I should tuck a couple of napkins into the neck of my shirt."

"You'll still find a way to get it on your shirt," Jess joked from the far end of the table. "Way to think things through, Eric."

The party quieted as everyone ate. On his third bite of spaghetti, a few drops of sauce splashed and splattered onto his shirt. "There it is." He let out a self-deprecating laugh while he tried unsuccessfully to wipe the red stain out.

"It's fine." Vickie smiled and grasped his hand across the table. "I don't care if there's a stain on your shirt."

Alexis watched this unfold out of the corner of her eye.

She wanted to hold Will's hand too like they had at the game, but he kept his hands in his lap throughout dinner.

Between bites, he glanced sideways across the table at Vickie and stared intently. She sensed that he was watching her. Every so often, she would shoot him an ugly look and he would turn away.

As she bit into her chicken wrap, her fangs poked her in the tongue. "Really?" she muttered to herself with a mouthful of food. *What are my fangs doing out? I'm eating dinner with friends.*

She noticed Will staring at her again. The vampire touched her tongue to the tips of her fangs and they protruded a little more when she realized that Will could not stop watching her.

What is with this guy? What does he want with me? And why do I react this way to another high school kid?

After they had all pooled their money together for the meal, the group walked out of the restaurant and turned the corner to stroll to the dance.

"Hey, I never asked where the dance was." Vickie couldn't imagine where anyone would hold a dance in a school building.

"It's in the main gym. You know, where we had the pep rally?" Eric took her hand as they walked.

She looked at their hands and smiled at him. "Wait, the gym? That doesn't sound like it's much fun."

"No, they decorate it. There's always a big theme every year, so they put together all kinds of props and decorations. They make it look really nice. You won't even recognize it as the gym when we get there."

Vickie was still doubtful, but the closer they got to the

school, the more excited she became. For weeks, she had heard about how much fun Homecoming was and now, she would experience it for herself, firsthand.

When they walked through the front doors of the school building, they were met with a loud blast of music from the massive speaker system installed in the gym. Hundreds of well-dressed high school kids wandered excitedly in the upstairs lobby outside the room.

Vickie peered through the doors while everyone hung their coats. *Oh, the lights are off. And there are other, fancy lights in their place. It actually looks cool in there. I wonder what the theme is.*

"Does anyone know the theme?"

"Not yet," Eric said. "We'll know when we get in there."

As they walked through the doors, Alexis released an excited laugh. The other kids—except for Will—cheered.

Plastered on the walls were giant pictures of Franken-stein, The Mummy, and of course, Dracula. A backdrop with a large mannequin dressed as a werewolf gave kids a funny place to take pictures. In one corner, a photo booth stood with a large box of scary masks beside it.

In big letters painted on a banner hanging above the DJ, the words *MONSTER MASH* lorded it over the dancing crowd.

Fake spiderwebs, plastic spiders, and dozens of jack o'lanterns were scattered all over the large space.

"It looks fantastic." Alexis beamed. "What a fun idea."

The group warmed up with a little light dancing to the early music before Alexis wanted to get a drink at the punch bowl.

"Will, do you want to come with me?" He shook his head and she sighed.

"I'll go with you. I'm thirsty," Vickie said and rushed to catch up with her. The two of them made their way to the punch bowl and filled a few cups.

"Well, I guess you fit in fine at this dance," Alexis joked. "Do whatever you want and no one will care."

"Very funny," the vampire replied. "I'm having so much fun with Eric. He's so sweet and a lot of fun to dance with."

"That's good." Her sister clearly wasn't having a good time.

"Are you all right?"

"I'm fine. Don't worry about me. Besides, I don't want to bring the party down for you. I'm really glad you're having fun. Really."

"Is it Will?"

Alexis blinked a few times, trying to keep the tears from welling up in her eyes. "Seriously, don't worry about it and have fun. I should have come with the girls."

She cleared her throat and walked away quickly as she tried to shake the sadness off and pretend to enjoy herself for the sake of the group.

"Hey, Alexis, you're a holiday girl, right?" Jamie smiled as she returned to the dance floor. "This must be heaven for you."

"Meh, call me when they do a Christmas-themed one." They all laughed and continued to dance.

Vickie and Eric danced together, but she constantly looked off to the side.

"Is something wrong?" he asked. "You seem distracted."

She shook her head. "No, I'm fine." A few minutes later, she glanced away again.

Will lingered on the border of the dance floor. He stood with his arms folded and glared at her while she danced.

The music changed to a slow song and Eric and Vickie stepped forward nervously. He rested his hands on her hips and she wound her arms around his neck. As the song progressed, they gradually stepped closer to each other.

She noticed that Alexis had finally persuaded Will onto the dance floor. As much as she hated him, she was happy to see that her sister would have at least one dance with him.

Finally, everyone is having a good time. Enjoy this, Vickie. Your first dance with your first date. You'll always remember this. She leaned forward and rested her head on Eric's shoulder.

A rush of nervousness pushed through him. Like any high school boy, the closer he got to the girl, the sweatier he became. He only hoped she didn't notice.

The vampire didn't notice at all. She closed her eyes and savored the moment. But when she opened them, she saw Will holding his date close…and still staring at her.

After the song, he walked away from Alexis and back to the side of the dance floor. A sad expression returned to the girl's face. She waved her arms and her hips to the more upbeat song that played and tried to either ignore or hide the fact that she was having a miserable time.

"Do me a favor," Vickie said to Eric. "Go dance with Alexis for a minute. I need to have a few words with Will." He gave her a curious look but slid over to Alexis and tried to cheer her up with a few goofy dance moves.

To Will's surprise, Vickie marched up to him, grabbed him by the arm, and dragged him out into the upstairs lobby of the school, away from the loud music.

"What is your problem?" she asked. "Why are you so infatuated with me?"

"I'm not," he said plainly. "I'm here to keep an eye on you."

"What does that mean?" She shook her hands at him in frustration. "What do you think I will do?"

He simply focused his vacant expression on her once more as her face grew almost crimson with rage. "I'm only doing my job."

"No, you're not. You're ruining a great dance for a great girl who deserves to have a great date. Why did you come with Alexis if you knew you'd pay no attention to her? That's not fair to her."

He had no answer.

She poked him in the chest with her finger. "She really likes you. Why, I have no idea, but she does. And she deserves to have a fun Homecoming Dance. If you can't do that for her, then leave. We'll make sure she has fun. And in the meantime, stop staring at me if you know what is good for you. You don't have to keep an eye on me."

Quickly, she closed her mouth without breaking her concentration. Her fangs threatened to emerge the more she yelled at him.

CHAPTER NINE

The rest of the dance went better. Vickie had mixed feelings as she watched Will dance with Alexis.

On the one hand, I'm happy to see her having a good time— and that trumps everything else. On the other hand, I hate that it's with him. I honestly wish he had simply left so we could have all danced together and perked her mood up.

Still, Will dancing with Alexis saved the night for everyone. Things were less awkward, the group laughed and had fun, and she could focus on her time with Eric.

The last song played at every school dance at Clear Lake High School was "Hey Jude" by The Beatles. As soon as Paul McCartney's voice echoed in the gym, the now-exhausted student body collapsed into each other's arms to savor the last dance of that year's Homecoming celebration.

Some groups circled to throw their arms around each other and sang at the tops of their lungs. This was especially true of the senior class, who used "Hey Jude" as a time to bond with the people they had been closest to for four years.

For the couples, it was an extended slow dance—a time to savor the romance a little longer before the lights came up.

Vickie and Eric cuddled, and so did Will and Alexis. Jess and Jamie slow-danced together and giggled all the way through it.

For the vampire, the song was a time to appreciate how well the night had gone. The drama with Will aside, she had a wonderful time with Eric. They had grown affectionate, held hands, and danced close all night long.

"Hey Jude" was the cherry on top of a great night.

Everyone's ears rang after the final notes faded away and the speakers were shut down. The lights in the gym came on again and warmed up gradually until they were bright once again.

She was surprised to see how few decorations there actually were. *I guess the secret to decorating a place like this is all the colored lights. What a difference they made.*

Eric returned from the bathroom as the group huddled together, waiting to decide what would happen next. "Guys, I talked to Brad. He's hosting an afterparty at his house in Muskego. We'll all need to catch rides down there."

"Awesome. I'm sure we can find someone to drive us. I'll text my dad and let him know where we're headed. He can pick us up there in the morning." Alexis fished her phone out from her purse and sent a hurried message to her father.

"Will his parents be there?" Vickie asked cautiously.

He smiled at her innocence. "Yes, they will. Brad's a good kid. He wouldn't throw a wild party or anything. Let's go."

The group split up to get rides down to Muskego that night. Alexis and Will rode with Todd Gehrke and Amanda Fuss. Todd was in Alexis' homeroom, so they knew each other well enough to take the fifteen-minute ride to Brad's house together.

Vickie was a little nervous. *I'll ride in someone else's car without Alexis. What if something happens and my fangs pop out? Or if I get scared and accidentally crush Eric's hand and shatter his bones into little pieces?*

Eric's friend, Bill Hart, offered to give them a ride. He was a good-natured boy who loved to laugh and was friendly to almost everyone he met. His girlfriend, who didn't go to Clear Lake, had partnered him to Homecoming. Together, the four of them traveled to Muskego.

During the drive, Eric and Vickie cuddled nervously in the back seat, where they shared their first kiss together. An intense feeling of warmth rushed to her cheeks afterward. They smiled awkwardly at each other, then held hands for the rest of the ride.

Most of Muskego was a rich part of town. Subdivision after subdivision cluttered the area and obnoxiously large houses lined the street, each one seemingly larger than the last.

Bill pulled his car into the circular driveway of a large two-story house illuminated by spotlights. He put it in park and turned. "We're here, lovebirds," he said with a laugh.

Brad Kook came from money, and his house showed it.

A heated in-ground pool occupied the back corner of an expansive lot. Just inside the patio door was an all-wooden room with a large hot tub for year-round soaking.

This almost looks like a castle. Vickie stared at the house in awe when they walked through the front door. Dozens of high school kids were scattered throughout, pounding sodas and having a great time.

Even though it was midnight, the party was only getting started.

To Vickie's relief, Brad led them through to the hot tub room, where his parents lounged on chairs watching the TV and keeping an eye on things. They were lovely people, friendly and welcoming.

As parents, they knew that this was the riskiest place in the house and they spent their evening in there to ensure that no misbehavior would take place. Anyone who wanted to sit in the hot tub needed to have a swimsuit on and no one would be left alone.

It was not a wild, misbehaving crowd, however. Brad was an A student, one of the top cross country runners on the boys' team and possibly the nicest person in the entire high school.

Eric and Vickie started upstairs in the game room, where a wall full of retro video games loomed over a foosball table, a pool table, and a small pair of basketball hoops.

"This looks interesting," she said and sidled up to the hoops. "What, you throw the balls into there?" She picked one of the basketballs up and tossed it through the hoop.

"Nice shot." He smiled at her. "Are you challenging me?"

For about fifteen minutes, the two of them competed playfully in game after game of basketball. Being a relatively strong athlete, Eric won every game, although he let her win the last one to be nice.

The two of them laughed and joked, and she could not stop smiling. *How lucky am I? I could have been killed centuries ago. Not only do I have a second chance at life, but I get to do it in a time when everything is amazing, and all the people are so nice and fun. This is the greatest thing ever.*

Her stomach twinged a little. Without looking, she turned to Eric. "I bet Will and Alexis are here."

Sure enough, her instincts did not lie. The two of them walked into the game room, holding hands. Alexis' face was flushed, and she seemed to wear a permanent smile.

After they had all greeted one another again, the two walked off to find something to drink.

"I have to tell you something," Alexis said tentatively, then rushed on to admit that Will had kissed her in the car on the way to the house. Vickie told her that Eric had done the same, and they celebrated their new boyfriends.

When her sister turned to select a drink, the vampire tempered her smile a little. *I'm so happy that she's happy. But man, I wish she had chosen someone better. I can't shake the feeling that there is something seriously wrong with that guy. But don't let it get to you right now. Let her have tonight.*

As the party wound down, Alexis didn't have too much time with her new boyfriend. While Brad was setting up a movie in the basement, Will told Alexis he had to leave.

"How will you get home?" she asked, bewildered. "You haven't called anyone. Do you have a ride?"

"I will be fine. Good night." He kissed her on the cheek and walked out the front door. She peered out the window and immediately noticed a waiting car—the same one that had dropped him off at their house at the beginning of the night. *How did they know to pick him up? I haven't seen him contact anyone all night.*

She did her best to ignore the sense of unease in her brain while she headed to the basement steps. It wasn't too difficult to spend the second half of the night pretending things were a lot better with Will. And they were—to a point.

But something about him was still a little off. She couldn't explain it either, but she had a guy who was showing interest in her. And for now, that was all that mattered. *It's not like I'm looking to get married tomorrow. Enjoy it. And hey, you still get to hang out with your friends tonight.*

When she reached the basement, her two friends were on the couch, his arm around her shoulders. She had snuggled in tightly, and they were getting comfortable before the movie started.

Alexis sat on the floor and leaned back against their legs. They dimmed the lights and started the movie—a comedy spoof of horror movies.

Vickie looked forward to seeing the jokes that would be made about vampires, but the next thing she knew, it was eight a.m. and she woke up on the couch. Other kids were sprawled everywhere. Eric was still in a seated position and Alexis lay at their feet.

Everyone had basically fallen asleep where they were. It had been a long night, but a fun one.

Vickie smiled and snuggled groggily to catch a little more sleep before the day began.

CHAPTER TEN

For Craig, Homecoming Night was a different story.

He parked the SUV in the garage and stood outside in his driveway to stare at the sky. Watching the stars made him think of his wife, who he imagined was dancing somewhere up in heaven—near the stars, he assumed.

The moon was full that night and bathed the outdoors in a soft glow. It was peaceful and serene. *After listening to all those high school kids chatter for twenty straight minutes, this is perfect.*

He walked over to the pool and rested his arms on it as he stared out at the field. A small frown settled between his brows when he looked down and noticed part of the pool's metal edge was bent and dented. *That almost looks like a handprint. What the heck happened here?*

Of course, he knew better than to ask too many questions.

Craig paced around the yard for a while, kicked the grass lightly with his feet, and enjoyed the quiet night.

Inside, however, he knew what he was really doing.

The girls would spend the night at an afterparty. He had the entire house to himself. Since Carol died, he hadn't spent an entire night there alone. He didn't know how it would feel—if it would be too uncomfortable, too lonely, or too unsettling.

All he knew was he really didn't look forward to it.

As he walked through the side door and turned the kitchen light on, he laughed at his foolishness. *When you were a bachelor, you lived alone like this for three years. No roommates and all the control in the world.*

He remembered the first year of their marriage when everything Carol did seemed to annoy him, from the way she did dishes to what TV shows she liked to watch. Craig loved having control over his environment. Marriage was a huge adjustment for him.

With a sigh, he turned on the living room lamp, which stood directly beside the curtains.

As a single man, he'd bought the cheapest curtains he could find. Simple colors with a basic rod that would serve its purpose and do nothing more. His wife taught him that it took a lot more than that to have a nice place.

Two weeks after they were married, she spent days poring through catalogs, going to stores, and finally getting the curtains she wanted, along with fancy curtain rods. For a solid hour, she ironed them in the living room while he took a drill and hung all the rods above the windows in their first apartment.

Once he was done, she had a neatly stacked pile of curtains that he was tasked to hang. One by one, he tried to hang them in each room of the house—only to discover that none of them fit the rods she'd purchased.

To him, it wasn't a big deal. But to her, it was days of work ruined. She fell to the floor and sobbed out of exhaustion while he laughed. He couldn't understand what the problem was.

After a few minutes, it stopped being funny. "Honey, get up. They're only curtains."

Craig smiled and shook his head as he recalled saying that. *Boy, was that the wrong thing to say to a crying woman.*

At the end of that night, he sat in a chair in their bedroom, rubbing his temples and terrified of what he had married.

Every day of their marriage, he learned a little more how to give up control of the environment. He was forced to allow her to set priorities and to support her when she tried to do things.

The days of coming home and plopping down on the couch for hours were over.

Now, as he stood in the living room and stared at those curtains, those very early days were back. He could sit in his recliner, watch three movies, and fall asleep.

But he missed helping her and trying to keep her from losing her mind. Most of all, he missed letting her take control of the place.

For years, he'd thought he would love to have that control again. He was wrong.

Maybe I can get some work done. I have to find a solution for this income situation anyway. He walked into his bedroom and sat at his desk.

It was a waste of time. He couldn't get his head to think

about work. All he could think about was the vacuum of the empty house.

When he didn't know what to do, he wrote. So, he pulled his journal out, turned it to a fresh page, and began writing:

After all these years, I've forgotten how to be alone.

It's amazing. I spent so much time alone in my adult life. I looked forward to the few times I could be alone after I got married and had Alexis. Now, I have an entire night to myself—and I don't want it.

I want Carol here. I want to eat dinner with her. I want to bicker with her over what movie we should watch together. I want to lose my patience with her when she pulls out her phone and plays games halfway through it. I want to place bets on who falls asleep first and collect my few bucks when I inevitably win.

I want to hear her snoring in her chair. I want to fight over the blanket with her.

But I don't get to do any of that anymore. Those days are gone, a distant memory in my mind and in my heart.

In its place is emptiness. Much like this house, I feel empty. When Alexis and Vickie are around, I can distract myself. And Alexis still fills part of me. She is now my life.

A large portion of my heart is simply sitting there, unused. I have no outlet for it. I have nothing to fill it with. And on nights like tonight, all I can do is embrace the discomfort and the pain.

I need to get used to this. The girls will be involved in high school activities, just like tonight. In a few years, they'll be off to college. I'll have this whole house to myself all the time.

Maybe I'll get used to it eventually. But tonight?

Tonight, I miss her. That's all.

Resolved to at least try to make the most of the evening,

Craig turned on the living room TV for a little background noise, then strolled into the kitchen to build himself a huge banana split.

He carried the bowl into the living room, sat in his recliner, and turned on one of his old favorite movies, *Tommy Boy*.

For two hours, he laughed hysterically, downed the ice cream, the chocolate, the cherries, the bananas, and the whipped cream, and told himself it was a well-rounded meal—even though he knew he would be awake at 3:00 am with a stomachache.

Afterward, he took the bowl into the kitchen and rinsed it in the sink. In his single days, he would think nothing of leaving it as it was overnight. Years of marital training had instilled in him the need to clean the kitchen before bedtime every night.

Around ten p.m, he felt drowsy. *There's no point in forcing yourself to stay awake. Get some sleep and you can enjoy a quiet breakfast before you go pick the girls up.*

Craig walked down the dark hallway and turned the bedroom light on again.

Instead of crawling into bed, he walked to the left side, where Carol used to sleep. He knelt beside the bed and fumbled beneath it to retrieve an old shoe box.

Carol had kept it for years. He knew she put her important treasures there, but she had never shared what was in it. *Now is as good a night as any to snoop around. Sorry, honey.*

With a tear in his eye, he smiled when he saw what was she had hoarded.

She was a sentimental woman, but she had a hard time preserving those memories. She wasn't very good at making photo albums or memory boxes. The old shoe box was all she had, and it was full of some good ones.

Lying on top was the letter Craig wrote to her after her cancer diagnosis. He'd wanted her to know exactly how he felt, but he didn't know how to say it out loud.

For a second, he considered reading it. As he unfolded it, however, he saw a few of the words and immediately folded it again. *That's a bad idea. Those words were for her, not for you. You'll only torture yourself if you read them again. Maybe another time. Not tonight, at least.*

He placed the letter to one side and resumed browsing through the box. A lock of Alexis' hair from her first haircut nestled in there, and a crude drawing of a dog and a bone. On the back of the paper, Carol had jotted, *Alexis' first art project from school.*

Even her handwriting made him feel warm inside.

A few dried, crackly flowers were tucked away in a corner. On closer inspection, he realized they were from their wedding. She had saved a few flowers from her bouquet.

Next to that was a matchbook from the Triton Hotel, where they spent their honeymoon. Under that, a movie stub from their first date.

Craig's lip quivered. He held a box in his hands that contained highlights of his entire life with his wife—from the moment they dated right up to her last days. All of it fit in the little shoe box that she moved from home to home—apartment to apartment to house—and always tucked away under her side of the bed.

He wondered how often she opened the box and when the last time she opened it was.

His heart heavy with nostalgia and the ache of grief, he tucked everything in the box except for the letter he wrote her, then returned it to its hiding place. He picked the letter up and put it on his dresser for later.

Finally, he turned and stared at the empty bed. For several months, he'd slept in it alone. *Not tonight.*

He turned away and walked into the living room, where he rearranged the throw pillows. After he'd retrieved a blanket from the wicker basket, he curled up on the couch and drew the coverlet under his chin.

Craig stared at the moonlight shining on the carpeted floor of the living room. *One step at a time. This is only Step One. You have a long way to go and more than enough time to get there.*

Good night, Carol, wherever you are. In case you're listening, I sure miss you right now.

CHAPTER ELEVEN

"Vickie, let's go. My dad's parked out front."

In the game room upstairs, Vickie and Eric held hands and said goodbye.

"Rrrrr…" Eric growled. "I don't want this weekend to end."

"I know." She smiled. "I had a great time with you. Thanks for being so much fun."

They both leaned in for a kiss. "Vickie. Let's *go!*" She turned to look at the door, then glanced back at him.

"I suppose I have to get going. See you at school?"

"Yeah. See you at school."

They kissed one more time. Both of them giggled and blushed before she ran downstairs to meet with Alexis and head to the car.

"Well? Did you two have a great time, or what?" Their father was excited to see them.

"It was great," Alexis replied with a not-quite-convincing tone.

"I loved it, but I'm exhausted." Vickie yawned loudly.

Craig laughed. "Oh yeah? Late night, eh? I remember those old high school afterparties. A good time, but they always made the next day drag because you stay up till sunrise having a good time together."

Alexis looked quizzically at her sister. "We weren't up that late. I think it was around two a.m. or something when we all fell asleep."

Her father shook his head. *Ah, when going to bed at two a.m. meant you were turning in early. To be young again.*

The vampire rested her head on the window. "Yeah, but by then, I was wiped out from keeping everything in check."

"What do you mean?"

"Sometimes, my instincts want me to do something. When those kick in, I have to concentrate really hard to not let my powers out. Otherwise, they'd come out naturally."

Alexis looked out the window and thought about the bruise on her shoulder. "Oh, we've noticed that."

"Vickie, do you think you need some kind of outlet for that?" Craig pursed his lips, his expression thoughtful. "Or can you...I don't know...simply tuck it away when that happens?"

She thought of the more than occasional late nights when she ran in the fields behind the house and bared her fangs in the cover of the night. "I do need an outlet for it, only to get it out of my system. Being a vampire is in my nature. That's hard to tuck away."

The gears began to turn in his head. "Okay. Good to know." *I wonder if I can come up with some kind of solution that would help her. A way she can burn energy safely and discreetly.*

"Plus, if you don't have an outlet for it, you wind up destroying the house and injuring people." Alexis winked at her.

"That's probably part of it," Vickie admitted. "I don't want to. I like being a normal American teenager. I'm having lots of fun. But I...uh, need to be a vampire sometimes."

"Of course you do—it's in your blood." Craig laughed.

His daughter groaned. "That was awful, Dad."

Later that afternoon, Alexis napped on the couch while Vickie snoozed in Carol's old recliner in the living room. He noticed they were both out cold, so he turned the TV off and pushed out of his chair. *The perfect opportunity. Let's see what I can dig out of the ol' shed.*

He opened the big garage door and backed the SUV out into the driveway. After he'd pocketed the keys, he flipped the switch to the overhead fluorescent light and made his way to the small add-on shed in the back of the garage.

I remember when Carol made me get rid of all this stuff. He moved a lawnmower and fertilizer spreader out of his way so he could get his hands on the big, brown leather punching bag tucked into the corner. *Little did you know, I kept it all and simply put it where you wouldn't look for it. Sorry, dear.*

A pair of boxing gloves and two rolls of wrist tape hung from a screw protruding from the wall. He retrieved both and put them on the workbench in the main area of the garage.

Craig then dragged a ladder to the middle of the

concrete floor, slung a heavy chain over his shoulders, and climbed up a few steps until he could reach the wooden rafters. He looped the chain carefully around the beams a few times and let the ends hang loose.

I used to hang this in my basement. Even putting it up and taking it down was a workout back then.

He flipped a five-gallon bucket, wrapped his arms around the punching bag in a big bear hug, and hoisted it onto the bucket. With a long stretch as high as he could reach, he connected the straps of the heavy bag to the chain to suspend it.

Now to give it a little test. He picked it up one more time to kick the bucket out of the way, then released it. The chain bore the weight easily, and it swayed freely. He assumed a fighting stance, danced around the bag, and threw haymakers at it for about ten seconds.

I'm already drenched in sweat. I forgot why I liked to do this so much.

He wiped his brow and let the bag dangle to sway lightly as the last of its momentum slowly faded. *What else can I put in here? The weights?*

Craig returned to the shed and dragged out a full barbell set. He laughed as he found a place for them. *I can't picture Vickie doing squats or anything, but maybe this will give her a little more opportunity to use that strength of hers.*

Finally, he located a small black vinyl bag that hung around the corner in the shed. *Oh, I forgot about these. They could work, too.* He ripped the velcro enclosure open to reveal a series of color-coordinated resistance bands.

Satisfied with his progress, he selected the heaviest one

and connected it to an anchor he placed in the doorway. *It'll give her some variety. That's good.* He quickly added the others to complete the available options.

He took a step back to survey the little home gym he'd crafted with real satisfaction but paused and stroked his chin. *Something is missing.*

After a moment or two of thought, he snapped his fingers when he realized exactly what it was he wanted. He had to crawl on all fours to reach a long piece of plywood under the other car. The size was perfect and he flipped it and found a half-empty can of black spray paint on the workbench.

With a goofy smile on his face, Craig sprayed a few words on the piece of timber. He lifted it up and propped it on the workbench so it was visible.

Much better.

About an hour later, both girls woke up and he asked them eagerly to come outside. "Come on, I have something to show you."

Alexis rolled her eyes. "Dad, can't this wait? We just woke up."

"Come on…you'll love it. It's a special surprise."

Vickie's eyes lit up. She liked surprises. "Let's do it." She scrambled to her feet and walked with him to the garage, while her sister trailed slowly behind and muttered something about no consideration.

He stepped in the middle of the garage and stretched his arms wide. "Ta daaaa!"

The vampire frowned at him, then studied all the equipment lying around. "Oh…it's nice."

Craig leaned forward. "That's it? Nice? That's all you have?"

"I guess I don't really know what it is."

"Vickie, this is your new gym. Use it as a place where you can unleash your powers whenever they are itching to get out."

A curious Alexis stumbled out of the house. Her eyes widened when she saw what he had done to the garage. Then, she saw the sign he painted.

"Does that seriously say, 'Vampire Gainz?' Dad, you are embarrassing."

"What? It's a vampire gym, what do you expect? Excuse me for having a little fun with it. Come on, let me show you around."

At each makeshift station, he showed Vickie what each exercise apparatus was for. He threw a few punches at the punching bag, demonstrated how to lift the weights, and showed her proper form with using the resistance bands.

His daughter stood in the background with her arms folded. "This will never work, Dad."

"Why not?"

"Vickie's not only strong, she's *super*-strong. She'll destroy this stuff." Her dad looked around with his hands on his hips, a slightly disappointed look on his face. He was clearly proud of his efforts. "You know what? Maybe I'm wrong, but we should at least test it. Vickie, do you want to give it a shot?"

She shrugged. "I guess so. I'm a little self-conscious, though."

"Well, this is for when you feel like you are itching to

use your powers. If you don't feel it right now, we can come out later." He gave the heavy bag a little tap.

The girl took a deep breath and closed her eyes. As her body relaxed, she felt a trace of her vampire tension build up inside her. "No, maybe I can do a little right now. I am getting antsy."

"That's what I figured." Craig hopped with excitement. "Where do you want to start?"

She pointed to the heavy bag. "That thing."

"Perfect." He clapped briskly. "First, we need to prepare your hands."

"Should she wear workout clothes for this, Dad?"

"Nah, she's wearing a t-shirt and sweatpants. That'll do fine." He bound her wrists carefully as she bounced on her heels in anticipation. "What is this for?"

"It's to protect you from breaking your wrists," he explained. "It's also a good way to remind you to keep your wrist straight when you punch the bag. If you go in crooked, you'll do considerable damage." He shoved the gloves over her hands. "These will cushion the blow."

Alexis smiled, shook her head, and took a few steps back while the two of them sidled up to the heavy bag. *I saw what she did to a car. That bag doesn't have a chance.*

Craig stepped behind the bag and held it steady for her. "Let's start with a few light jabs. Get your feet moving and don't try to kill the thing. Just make contact and get comfortable."

Vickie did as she was told and punched the heavy bag with a force she considered light. When she made contact, it pounded into Craig's gut and knocked the wind out of him.

"Are you okay?" she asked as he coughed.

"I'm fine." He was not convincing and clutched his chest as if to contradict himself. "I think the bag will be fine. I'll stand behind you. Now, go ahead."

She threw a few more jabs at the bag and it rocked and swayed violently.

"Good. Now give me a solid hit with all you've got."

Alexis cringed. *Here we go.*

Vickie felt her vampire blood flow through her body. Her brain sent signals to the rest of her that it was okay to go full force. She swung and punched the bag so hard, the seams split and it literally exploded. Sand erupted everywhere and piled on the garage floor. She stood frozen in her fighting stance with a spooked look on her face.

Alexis laughed. "I told you, Dad."

He waved his hand in the air to clear the dust. "Maybe punching was a bad idea. How about lifting? How strong do you get?" He helped her remove the gloves and tape from her hands.

"I don't know," she said. "I haven't really measured."

"Dad, seriously, put all the weights on there."

"All of them?"

"Every last one. You've seen what she's done to solid metal. Trust me."

When he remembered the car handle incident in Salzburg, Craig slid every weight onto the barbell. He stepped back and stared at it. "This is like four hundred pounds."

"She's got it, Dad. Go for it, Vickie."

Feeling a little like a coach, he crouched, his hands on his knees, as he gave her a little pep talk with instructions.

"Let's try a deadlift. That's really safe, really simple, and we don't have to go crazy with it. Bend over, grab the bar, lift with your legs, and stand straight."

"That's it?"

"That's it." He patted her on the back. "Go for it."

Now that she had really got her blood moving, the vampire felt the power course through her limbs even more. She grasped the bar, stood, and lifted it off the ground. Unfortunately, she was so strong that it launched upward and crashed into the rafters above her head.

Vickie jumped out of the way, and Craig grabbed his daughter and pulled her to safety.

The airborne equipment shattered a sheet of plywood that spanned the rafters. A pile of lawn chairs stored for the winter plummeted, along with the barbell. The sand-filled weights cracked and made an even bigger mess.

The three of them stood in stunned silence for about twenty seconds, unable to process what exactly had happened.

Alexis was the first to break the silence. "Do you want her to try the resistance bands next?"

Her father walked over to the side door and removed the anchor and the bands wedged in them. "Probably not. I'll clean this up and we'll have to think of something else. You girls go on in."

Vickie felt wired with energy, but as the levels increased, so did the tightness in her stomach. "There it is again."

"What?" Alexis asked as they walked up the driveway.

"That feeling. Something is wrong. I wish I knew what

this meant. There's something bad out there and I don't even know where to look."

The other girl opened the side door. "Your parents never taught you about that stuff?"

She shook her head, frustrated. "I don't know. I don't think so. If they did, I don't remember, anyway."

CHAPTER TWELVE

T he bell rang through the hallways for first lunch. Vickie stood from her desk and smiled with excitement.

The break was a time to hang out with Eric. They could talk, eat, and enjoy each other's company without really thinking about school. But today was a little more special because they could drop the flirting. They were official.

Wait...are we? We kissed a couple of times. He was really affectionate with me all weekend. But we didn't talk about it. Are you supposed to talk about it?

He waited outside her classroom for her so that they could walk to lunch together—another new perk of the relationship. She greeted him with a big smile, and they strolled to the cafeteria.

They dropped their bags at the usual table and headed to the food line together. Neither of them had much to talk about, so she dealt mainly with awkward silences.

Eric, for his part, was crippled with self-consciousness. *I've never had a girlfriend before. How am I supposed to act around her? Should I have my arm around her all the time? Would that be annoying? If not, what am I supposed to do with my hands? Does my hair look stupid? I should've checked it before I met up with her but now, it's too late to do anything about it.*

After they'd filled their trays and paid for their food, they returned to the table where Jess waited, already several bites into her sandwich.

"Hey, lovebirds," she greeted them.

The two of them exchanged a nervous laugh as they sat. This time, however, Eric sat next to Vickie instead of beside Jess on the other side of the table.

"Ohhhh…" Jess chuckled when she noticed. "A new arrangement. Well, good. I was tired of watching you two stare at each other. It made it hard to keep my lunch down."

"Oh, ha-ha." He laughed sarcastically. "No one's stopping you from finding a boyfriend. Now, there's a spot open in the chair next to you. Be our guest and fill it."

"Yeah, right. I don't want to spend lunch worrying about whether or not there's food in my teeth. I'll simply sit here and enjoy the freedom, thank you very much."

Vickie turned away and tried to look casual as she ran her tongue along her front teeth. *I didn't think of food in my teeth. Is that bad? Have I had food in my teeth this whole time?*

"Anyway, when will you two go out on a date?" the other girl asked as she picked up her can of soda.

The couple looked at each other again and each tried to gauge the other's reaction. "We haven't talked about it," Eric replied, his voice wavering. "Hey, slow down. We spent all weekend together. When would we have had time to plan a date?"

"A date would be fun." Vickie smiled and focused on her milk carton. "I'd like that."

His stomach did somersaults. He wasn't ready to discuss going out on a date. It was something terrifying because he had no money to treat her, no car to take her, and no clue what girls liked to do on a date.

Like most high school boys, Eric wasn't even sure she wanted to go on a date with him—and even after she said she did, he still doubted her.

The silence hung in the air like a heavy blanket dropped over them. He had to react, and she would surely expect him to come up with a date idea. Eric wasn't one to thrive under pressure, so he said the first thing that popped into his head.

"Maybe we could go with Will and Alexis somewhere. You know, double-up?"

Jess sat slack-jawed with a slight smile. *That's the best you got, Eric? Strong start.*

"I don't know if it's a great idea." Vickie gritted her teeth. "Will isn't exactly a…" Her voice trailed off. She didn't know how to end that sentence.

"Will's a jerk." Jess wasn't one to mince words. "Come on. We all went out with them on Saturday. The guy is no fun, has zero personality, and won't talk to anyone. Right, Vickie?"

Whenever his name came up, her mind immediately recalled the afternoon when he'd told her that he hated her and he didn't know why. They were mortal enemies, and his obsession with her made her uncomfortable.

It was more than that, though. He brought out the vampire in her. As Jess and Eric debated the merits of the boy, she stewed silently in her thoughts. Her stomach twisted and her legs twitched with energy.

"I don't know about Will," Vickie said to him. "There's something about him. I can't explain it but I worry about Alexis and him."

Eric, ever the oblivious high school boy, gave her a quizzical look. "They seemed fine at Homecoming. He was probably only nervous. You know, new kid in school and all."

"I'm a new kid in school." Vickie placed her hand on her chest. "I had a blast."

"Sure, but you know us. You're family with Alexis, and you met all of us over the summer. So you're comfortable."

Jess nodded. "He's got you there. Will was in a group he was unfamiliar with. I merely think he's a big, dull dud, that's all."

The vampire took a bite of her chicken and shook her head. "I think he's bad for Alexis, and something tells me he's dangerous."

The other girl winced at that word. "I don't know if I'd describe him as dangerous. That might be a step too far."

Eric agreed. "He might be shy or self-conscious. There are many reasons why a dude might act like that at a school dance that have nothing to do with him actively trying to be a jerk."

All this talk about Will had Vickie roiling with suppressed power. *This isn't the cool, relaxing lunch I envisioned spending with my boy. Do we have to talk about Will the whole lunch?* "Let's change the subject."

"Yeah, okay. So I have a question." Jess gave her a curious look. "What's up with your teeth?"

"My teeth?" She hadn't noticed because she was so thoroughly worked up, but her fangs had begun to emerge. They hadn't fully extended, but the points narrowed and protruded barely enough to be visible from across the table.

She covered her mouth with her hand. "Oh, I think I have some food stuck in them."

Jess shook her head, puzzled. "No, they look totally different. Here, let me see." She leaned forward to get a closer look.

Vickie almost leapt from the table, her hand still covering her mouth. "Um…no, you know what? I was just… I had to see a…tooth doctor yesterday…" *Good grief, why can't I remember the word for one of those?*

"The dentist?" Eric asked, wide-eyed.

"Yeah, the dentist. That's what I meant, the dentist. I saw the dentist yesterday."

"What kind of dentist does work on Sundays?"

Oh, yesterday was Sunday. That's right. "It was a special visit. An emergency. Yep, emergency dental work on my front teeth. They're still a little sensitive. He told me they could get a little pokey while they heal."

Eric scratched his head. Jess looked at him to see if any of this made sense to him.

"Yeah, so, I should actually go check the mirror in the bathroom and see if they're getting better."

He raised a finger. "If you had emergency dental work done yesterday, why didn't you say anything until now? It seems like something you would bring up a lot sooner."

She waved her other hand frantically in an attempt to pass it off as no big deal. "I didn't want attention. You know how it is. Anyway, I gotta go." She snatched her backpack and scuttled through the cafeteria, leaving her tray behind at the table.

By the time she reached the entrance to the cafeteria, she felt her fangs retract. Her body was distracted enough to calm. *Great. But now that I've run off like a crazy person, I can't go back and pretend nothing happened. And if they keep talking about Will, they'll come back. Ugh, why does this vampire stuff have to be so complicated?*

Because she said she would look in the bathroom mirror, Vickie decided she could kill a little time by following through with it. She stepped into the bathroom and found a place at one of the mirrors over a sink.

After a furtive glance around to confirm that she was alone, she leaned forward and pulled up her lips up slowly to check her fangs. *Whew, okay. They're definitely gone now. Good.*

She released a deep breath to relax. Unfortunately, she had been so preoccupied with her teeth that she didn't notice Megan Fitz sitting on the couch in the corner. The girl watched her intently.

"What, you got food in your teeth or something, Frau? Not a good look when you're sitting with your boyfriend."

Oh, great. "Hey, Megan."

She flashed an insincere smile. "How's the car coming along?"

"It's early. I haven't started it yet."

"Ooh...working from behind. You like to work under pressure, eh? Mine's already done."

Vickie turned back to the mirror. "I didn't ask."

"My brother and I are testing it at home. I think we'll break the all-time distance record. I might go to Goodwill this weekend and start shopping for your new winter outfit."

"Don't get too confident yet, Megan." She poked at her fang teeth with her index finger while she stared in the mirror. "There is more than enough time left."

"Well, to warn you, my car is already reaching a hundred feet." She stood and stretched her legs.

"A hundred feet?"

"Yep. And wouldn't you know it, that's only thirteen feet away from the all-time record. My brother and I will tweak the design, make the adjustments, and we'll destroy whatever piece of garbage you bring to the big day."

Vickie had no plans for her car yet, but she wanted to make sure her adversary knew she wouldn't back down. "I have the blueprints drawn up. I don't need anyone's help. I'll double that all-time record."

"Double? Oh, sweetie...if you want to talk trash, you need to at least be a little more realistic. If you double the record, my car will fly to the moon and back."

She walked out of the bathroom with a loud, mocking laugh.

The vampire took a step back and scowled at herself in the mirror. "You'd better have some idea up your sleeve, or she'll embarrass you again."

During physical science the next morning, Mr. Bilitz stood in front of the room and beamed at the class.

"When I announced the end of semester competition, I said there would be a prize for the winner. Today, it's time to let the cat out of the bag." He reached into his pocket and pulled out a small envelope, which he held over his head. "The one who designs the longest-traveling car in the class will win this one-hundred-dollar Amazon gift card."

The classroom cheered. Megan and Vickie made eye contact. The other girl's eyes were wide and she raised her eyebrows, impressed. *The stakes have been raised, Frau. Now, I get to humiliate you and win me some spending money.*

CHAPTER THIRTEEN

That Friday afternoon, Vickie sat on the grass at Hart Park with the other cross country girls, stretching her legs.

She was preparing for her first Varsity race and she was excited. She could run a touch faster if she wanted to, and she had really bonded with some of the older girls. Shannon, the team captain, respected her and welcomed her onto the team. Krista had become her closest friend during practices.

Now, she could race with all the girls.

Coach Lueck walked past them and clapped. "New day, new race, girls. Who's excited?" They smiled politely and a few of them waved their hands to pacify his enthusiasm. "You can do better than that. Come on. This is racing weather. We'll have some fun today. Vickie, can I talk to you for a minute?"

The vampire nodded, stood quickly, and jogged over to her coach, who put his hand on her shoulder.

"How are you feeling today? Loose? Relaxed? Are you nervous at all?"

"No, sir. I feel good. I think I'll do well today."

That was the answer he wanted to hear. "Atta girl. This is only your second race and you're on the Varsity team now. Don't let yourself get psyched out. This is the same kind of race as the last one, except you'll probably be closer to the middle of the pack instead of winning the race. This isn't for any championships or anything. We're only trying it out today but I'd like to see a little aggressive racing out there. And have some fun because this is fun, right?"

"Sure."

He nodded and sent her back to the team for more warm-up. Shannon laughed.

"Coach really likes race days. They get him all excited. The guy waits all year to get to coach some races."

"It's okay." Vickie sat, extended her leg, and stretched to touch her toes. "He likes his job. There's nothing wrong with that. I'd rather have him be too happy than too grumpy."

The girls ran-walked the course to warm up and get a feel for the park. Coach joined them to provide relevant details and tips.

"There are a fair number of flat stretches here, girls, with enough room to battle. I expect some fast times today. Hills are few and far between."

They reached a wooded area with thick trees on both sides.

"This is another stretch where you'll do some racing," he explained. "It gets a little tight here, so stay safe. Don't let anything distract you from the race. Focus on the runners in front of you and get after it."

After the warmup, they removed their outer gear and headed to the starting line.

Shannon gave Vickie an encouraging smile. "Are you ready, rookie?"

"Oh yes." *I only hope I keep a believable pace.*

The starting gun fired and the ladies started their watches as the race began.

Vickie had a simple goal for the event. Be competitive but be the last player on the team. She wanted to make sure she made a good showing that would keep her on Varsity. At the same time, though, she didn't want to suddenly outrun all the other members of her team who had worked very hard to get as far as they had.

In the days before the race, Coach Lueck had told her he wanted her in the "fifth man" role. As he explained to her, in cross country, the final standings for the first five runners on the team were tallied. The team with the lowest overall number won the meet.

And as he was fond of saying, "A team is only as good as their fifth man. If your first four runners go one-two-three-four in the race, but your fifth runner comes in ninety-seventh, your team lost. The fifth man has to be competitive."

The vampire loved the idea. She could run well, contribute to the team, and not steal the limelight from the leading runners like Shannon. The role allowed her to simultaneously be important and to blend in.

As the race progressed, she kept a close eye on her

teammates and made sure to stay well behind the fourth girl.

Stick to the plan today. Many runners seem to have an extra kick when they get close to the finish line. Pace yourself and stay well behind, and you can outrun some of the other girls as you finish. Nice and easy.

Coach was right about the course. It was fast. She kept pace with the other girls and her splits were almost thirty seconds faster than her last race. During the first flat stretch, he jogged alongside her just off the course.

"Vickie, you're coming out strong. Make sure you're not too strong. If you can keep this pace, then work it. But if this is faster than you can run, back off a little. Conserve your energy if you have to. There is still most of the race left."

She nodded and tried to look like she was concentrating hard and pushing herself. When he was out of view, she relaxed her face again and appeared as though she was out for a light jog.

Vickie reached the patch of trees with a handful of other girls in the middle of the race. For a few moments, she felt serene. The trees were lovely, the sun was shining, and it really was a great race day.

She ran alongside a short blonde girl from Hartford High School who appeared to be running very hard to keep up. But for Vickie, it was all rather relaxing.

Then she felt a sharp sting on the side of her calf. She stumbled and fell face-first into the dirt.

What the heck was that? She looked down at a thick trickle of blood running down her leg. A closer look confirmed a puncture wound in her calf. *Seriously?*

"Hey!" she shouted down the path. Other runners turned to look at what was going on. She pumped her legs and caught up with the Hartford runner. "What was that for? I'm only trying to race here."

"Yeah, and I'm trying to win. Quit crying." The girl puffed between her sentences, then threw her foot sideways and kicked Vickie again in the calf. She fell even harder that time.

She sat up and looked at her leg, which was now covered in blood. Her uniform was caked with dirt and old mud. She wiped some of the dirt off her face and noticed there was more caked on her forehead and in her hair.

Anger bubbled up inside her. She sprinted down the line to catch up with the girl.

Her rival wasted no time and kicked her again. This time, Vickie was ready for her and gave her a little push, careful to not overpower her instinctively.

The girl regained her balance and swiped viciously again. *Ugh, enough of this!*

With nearly a hundred yards to go in the wooded area, Vickie closed her eyes, allowed her super-speed through, and bolted away as quickly as a bullet leaving the chamber of a gun.

Most of the other girls were looking at the ground to watch their footing and didn't even notice her. But a hundred yards back, the Hartford girl looked around to see if she was the only one who saw what had happened.

This extra sprint closed the gap between Vickie and the fourth runner on the girls' team. "Come on, let's do this," she encouraged her teammate, who was sucking wind and running out of energy.

The two ran side-by-side until they saw the finish line. "Go get it," she shouted to the girl, who surged forward with every last ounce of energy she had left in her legs.

The vampire ran a few paces behind her and eased her speed so the other girl would cross the finish line first.

When they stopped, they hugged in exhaustion—one girl's real, the other girl's feigned—and moved down the chute to have their numbers taken.

The girls' team high-fived and hugged, then cheered Vickie for her excellent race.

"Whoa! Are you okay?" Krista pointed to her bloody calf and the mud spattered over the rest of her. "You look like you've been through a war."

"Yeah, I'm fine. It stings, but it's okay. Some girl in the woods actually kicked me. I couldn't believe it."

"Oh, yeah." Shannon nodded her head. "You were spiked."

"Spiked?"

"That's what dirty runners do when no one's looking. They kick you with the spikes on their racing shoes. It happens more often than you think."

I can't believe anyone would cheat so badly simply to do better in a race. "Have you all been spiked before?" Each girl nodded and most of them admitted to multiple injuries because of it. "Wow. Why would someone do that?"

Krista laughed. "It's something of a compliment, actually. It means you were annoying her by running as well as her—or better."

The girl from Hartford walked past the team and glared at Vickie. She was white as a sheet as if she had seen a ghost. The vampire met her gaze expressionlessly before her rival walked away to her team.

"That was her?" Krista asked. She nodded. "She's so little. No wonder she spiked you. Her legs are probably too short to run any faster. I bet that's her only plan for these races."

One of the assistant coaches helped Vickie clean and bandage her leg. She limped around the course to cheer Eric on during his race.

At the end of the meet, the Clear Lake Varsity girls' team won the gold. Coach pulled her aside.

"Vickie, that was one heck of a race out there today, and I am so proud of you. You went after it, raced hard, and even took a few hits for the team. That's the kind of heart I want to see from all my runners. Keep this up and you'll be a shoo-in for team captain in a couple of years. For now, know that you were incredible today. Well done."

She closed her eyes and smiled. *He's proud of me. I'm doing something right here.*

Finally, it was all over. She grabbed her bag and met Eric in the line for the bus, where they would snuggle up on the ride back to the high school.

Even though she was filthy and bleeding, it had been a good day for Vickie Hewitt.

CHAPTER FOURTEEN

"Are you ready for choir practice?" Jamie walked up to Jess as she threw her backpack in her locker.

"Hooray for concert season." Jess' voice dripped with annoyed sarcasm.

The Fall Concert was a few weeks away—the first opportunity for parents to see what their kids had learned in choir at school. This meant a few extra practices, usually conducted after school let out on a weeknight.

She pulled her choir music folder off the top shelf and slammed the door shut. Her usual cheerful expression was sour when she spun and leaned up against her locker. "I like choir, but ugh, I can't stand extra practices. We have enough things to do."

Jamie shrugged. "It beats having an extra class during the day."

Choir was considered a class at Clear Lake. During the fourth period every day, the choir got together in the Choir Hall and practiced. If the director felt the singers weren't getting enough practice during that period, he scheduled additional mandatory practices after school.

Jess rifled through her folder to make sure she had all the pieces of music they would rehearse. "Hey, so we never talked about this… Does Vickie seem…weird to you?"

"How so?"

"I don't know. I keep getting this weird vibe from her." She closed her folder and they began walking down the hall. "Like when she threw you in the pool?"

"Yeah, that made me uncomfortable." The girl nodded her head and waved to a friend on the other side of the hall. "I didn't really care that she reacted the way that she did. I thought we were all having fun, but maybe her culture doesn't really do that. But her *strength*. That surprised me."

"I legit have never seen someone thrown that far before," Jess said. "You were so far up in the air, I thought you would be seriously hurt by the time you hit the water."

Jamie shook her head. "It was scary. *So* scary. And like, she apologized and I'm sure she didn't mean to do it. But how do you get that strong in the first place?"

"She's a runner. It's not like she does any lifting. Or working out at all."

The other girl curled her lip. "I read a story once about a woman who lifted a car off her son who was under it, right? Her kid was dying, so she ran over there, pushed up on the bumper, and picked the car up off the ground. They said it was an adrenaline thing. Like, it gives you super-strength or something."

"So you think that's what happened?" Jess was skeptical of this conclusion.

But Jamie was nice to a fault. She wouldn't make any rash judgments about someone, especially a friend. "That's the best reason I can give. Have you thought about that this whole time?"

"No. Only since lunch."

"What happened at lunch?"

"We were talking about Alexis and Will."

Jamie rolled her eyes. "Oh, geez. Alexis deserves so much better than that guy."

"He is cute."

She waved the statement off impatiently. "Who cares? He's only a bump on a log. I get the feeling that Alexis is stuck with him. She wants a boyfriend so badly, and when he asked her out, she couldn't say no. I don't think she had fun at Homecoming."

Jess gave her an amused look. "So you're not a fan of the guy, eh? That says a lot coming from you."

"What's that supposed to mean?" She was almost offended and she didn't even know what she was being accused of.

"You simply give people the benefit of the doubt."

"And that's a bad thing?"

"It's a little goody-goody, that's all. Anyway, we were talking about getting the four of them on a double date. Eric is terrified of doing the wrong thing around her, so I thought there would be strength in numbers."

"It's not the worst idea. I guess, if there were anyone but Will involved, it would be a great idea." Jamie was fiercely protective of her friends. Despite her accepting nature, she never tolerated anyone who hurt them.

"Apparently, you and Vickie have that in common. She was really getting upset by it."

"So? Is that weird? I'd be upset too."

Jess stopped and pulled her friend off to the side before they reached the Choir Hall. "Yeah, but her teeth…looked like they were changing."

The girl frowned in bewilderment. "Changing? How?"

"Like…they got pointier. Only these." She pointed to her fang teeth.

"She was growing fangs?" Jamie burst out laughing. "That's not at all where I expected this conversation to go."

"I'm telling you, I saw her fangs get pointy. She made up some excuse about food being in her teeth and whatever and ran off."

Jamie could tell the girl was sincere in her description—and it wasn't the type of thing she would lie about in the first place. "I don't know. That sounds a little far-fetched. Maybe there really was food in her teeth. How do you grow fangs?"

"What am I, a dentist?" Jess demanded, more than a little exasperated. "I've spent all day trying to make sense of this, and I've come up with nothing."

Her friend stared at the ground as she tried to think of a logical reason for all of this. "So she's…like, a werewolf or something." She laughed. "Maybe there was a full moon outside the cafeteria."

Jess rolled her eyes and walked on ahead.

"Oh, come on, Jess! What do you want me to say? It's not like I don't believe you. But I don't know…do we confront her? Do we ask Alexis? What?"

"I don't know either." She sighed.

They walked into the choir room, where kids milled about around four long rows of black chairs. The director hadn't arrived yet.

"You know what's my favorite part of these after-school choir practices?" Jess asked as she glanced at the clock.

"What?"

"We're supposed to be here at 3:30 on the dot. It's 3:30 and Mr. Goede's not even here yet. It's okay for him to be late."

Seconds later, a short, pudgy man with glasses and a wispy mustache walked in with a smile on his face. "Who's ready to sing?"

The kids took their places. Jess and Jamie stood next to each other in the alto section.

Two hours later, everyone emerged from the choir room, exhausted. Their voices cracked from so much effort.

"I was thinking during practice…" Jamie said tentatively.

"Yeah?"

"Maybe Vickie is a little weird. Remember when Alexis told us she was going to Salzburg?"

"Of course." Jess, Jamie, and Eric had taken Alexis to a movie a few days after her mom's funeral. It was a kind gesture from friends who wanted to help her move on from mourning, at least for a few hours.

After the movie was over, they stopped at Gilles' for frozen custard. While seated at the table enjoying chocolate waffle cones, Alexis broke the news to them that she and her father would be going to Salzburg.

"Do you remember her ever saying she had family in

Salzburg?" Jamie asked. "She said they were going there because it was a cheap castle in the middle of nowhere, right?"

Jess scanned her memory with a frown before she nodded. "You're right, she never said anything about having family in Salzburg."

The other girl grew excited. She felt like a detective pulling at a thread to unravel a mystery. "And she was there for over a month before suddenly, this Vickie girl is there."

"Right. And she never mentioned having family in Austria—ever. That doesn't mean it can't be true, but it's a little weird that they went there at random and came home with a cousin. Do you think she's lying?" Jess didn't like that thought. It would make sense, but it would also mean their friend was in danger.

"I don't know. If Vickie's lying about that, how would she have proven it? I can't imagine Alexis' dad simply saying, 'Oh, gee, you say you're family? Come home with us.' There must have been some kind of proof or…something. Anything."

Another thought crossed the other girl's mind. "Adding to that…Vickie's from Austria. But no accent?"

Jamie's eyes widened. "Yes. I've thought of that, too. She should sound like Arnold Schwarzenegger or something. She lived there her whole life but doesn't have an accent? That one kid who moved here from Texas still has a southern accent and he's lived here for two years."

They stopped at each other's lockers to put their music things away and retrieve their bags before they continued quietly down the halls. Neither of them wanted to really admit that they thought Vickie was a fraud. Deep down, they didn't believe that.

But neither of them could make heads or tails out of all this conflicting information. After a short walk, they reached the back door, where Ashley would be waiting with the car.

"It seems too wild to even bother," Jess said. "I don't want to think about it. Alexis would know better than anyone."

"I know." Jamie admitted she didn't want to think that way either. "But I don't want to see Alexis hurt. There's probably a simple explanation for all of this that we've overlooked."

"We'll ask her about it. See what she says."

They exchanged a hasty glance and turned on their heels. Ashley would wait, and this wouldn't take long. The girls found Alexis in the upstairs lobby.

"Hey, is Vickie around?" Jess asked as she walked up to their friend.

"No, she has cross country practice. What's up?"

They drew her to the side of the lobby, away from the heavy traffic of students who tried to get out of the building as quickly as possible.

"We want to know what's up with Vickie." Jamie leaned in with a concerned look on her face.

"What do you mean?" Alexis' heart stopped. *Are they catching on? Did Vickie slip up too much around them? Shoot. What can I say?*

The girls presented their concerns—the pool incident and her fangs showing at lunch. Alexis listened only partially as her mind raced through options for how to explain it all away.

A wave of panic rushed over her and she began to sweat as her nerves tingled.

"I see her every day. I live with her, and I haven't noticed anything like that." *I hate lying to my best friends. But I have to protect Vickie somehow.* "You know, in the pool, I think that had to do with adrenaline. Before we went swimming that day, she told me she had never really gone swimming before. When you two dunked her, she panicked, that's all."

"But she threw Jamie, like, a few feet in the air," Jess pointed out, her face pinched with skepticism. She didn't like her friend's answer.

"You don't know that. Sometimes, it seems like something is way worse than it actually is, right? In the heat of the moment, it probably looked like she was launched way in the air. You only remember it how it felt instead of how it was."

The girls knew there was no way to disprove that theory. "But what about her teeth?" Jess asked. "I clearly saw them poke out. It was like she had fangs or something."

Alexis shrugged and made a valiant attempt to put on as convincing a show as she could. "Who knows? Maybe the angle or the lighting you were in made it look that way. She could've had food in her teeth and it simply appeared like she had fangs."

Jess rolled her eyes. "That was her excuse, too."

"What are you trying to say?" *You'd better make this sound as ridiculous as possible, girl.* "You think she's a *vampire* or something?" She uttered a loud, fake laugh.

The other two looked at each other. "I guess it does sound a little ridiculous."

"What's more plausible, here? That maybe your eyes are deceiving you a little, or that Vickie is some creature of the undead whom we brought to America to go to high school?"

The girls smiled. "Yeah, you're right," Jamie said and nodded. "I think our imaginations maybe ran a little wild."

"Girls, trust me, if there was something up with Vickie, I would tell you about it. She has a few quirks because she was raised differently from you and me. The girl needs our support. I'm trying to guide her to know what it's like to look and act normally in our country. I could use your help."

They agreed and all parted amicably to go home. Jess and Jamie were not thoroughly convinced, as their skepticism remained high. But their brains couldn't logically dispute the counter-arguments, so they had to let it go.

As she walked to the door, Alexis released a deep breath and tried to stop sweating. *Okay, you dodged that bullet. But you can't keep doing that. This won't end well.*

CHAPTER FIFTEEN

Hannes glanced at his watch. *22:57. Come on, hurry. They're waiting for you.*

He sprinted across the bridge that spanned the Salzach River and dodged couples in love who snuggled in the moonlight. *If you only knew what I knew.*

Fear gripped him and sweat rolled down the side of his face. Without thinking, he lifted the black cloth in his arms and dabbed his forehead with it. *Shoot. I wasn't supposed to do that. I hope no one notices. The lights will be low. It'll be okay. Just focus on getting there.*

On the other side of the Salzach, he accidentally ruined a family photo being taken in front of Mozart's Geburtshaus, where the composer first lived as a child. He didn't even realize that he ran through the picture. Even if he had known, there was no time to pause and apologize.

When he reached the Dom zu Salzburg, he stopped and resumed a normal walking pace and did his best to fit in with the people still around that late at night. Once he reached the front steps, he skipped up them two by two and pulled open the large, wooden door.

The cathedral was so quiet, all he heard was his heavy breathing from all the running. Normally, he liked to slip into the chapel area and light a candle, but there was absolutely no time. With a manila folder tucked under his arm, he hopped the barrier leading to the basement stairs and pulled the robe over his head.

He walked into the candle-filled crypt where Gabriel already stood in front of the group and presided over the meeting.

"You are late." The leader's stern voice sent a chill up Hannes' spine.

"Yes, sir." He swallowed and made an effort to slow his breathing.

The man extended his hand and gestured for him to come forward. His head ducked under the hood of his robe, he joined the circle.

"As you know, our righteous mission has been reignited before our very eyes." Gabriel took on a fierce, fire-and-brimstone tone of voice that would make any preacher proud. "We did not believe that this day would ever come. The evil our ancestors in the Circle exterminated from the world has been reborn. Brother Hannes, have you located the entity?"

Hannes licked his lips and opened the folder to shuffle through his papers. "Yes, sir. I believe I have located her."

"Proceed." The leader stepped aside and ushered him forward. Nervously, he stumbled to the front of the group. He stammered through his presentation of the research he had been tasked with. In all his years with the group, he had never spoken much at the meetings—he supported the mission but was more of a follower.

"I searched through online profiles and cross-examined all the information I could find that could be reasonably tied to her. My conclusion is that the vampire girl is currently alive in Milwaukee, Wisconsin, in the United States of America."

A murmur hummed through the group. Hannes held his breath. He couldn't confirm anything but he felt confident that his research was right. Some of the group audibly expressed their disbelief to each other.

One man raised his hand. "If the girl is, indeed, a vampire descendent, how could she have crossed the Atlantic Ocean? This does not make sense."

He nodded at the man. "I agree, but—"

"And what would make her go that far inland? There has to be something there. A reason for her travels."

Another man gasped. "You don't think that there are more of them, do you? That they are all gathering in Milwaukee, Wisconsin?"

Gabriel shook his head. "No, that would not be the case. There would be far more evidence to support that. Hannes, in your research, did you come across any evidence suggesting more than one vampire?"

"No, sir." He could answer that question with confidence. "She's alone. That is how we found her in the first place. The reason she posted online is because she wants to connect with other vampires."

"Then she is trying to organize it. She wants to assemble the vampire race once again."

The group argued loudly with one another for a while.

Gabriel stood on the far side of the room and stoically watched all this unfold. *This girl is bringing us nothing but disorder. We cannot work like this.*

At the front of the room, Hannes stood silently, his notes in hand, and waited for a break in the chaos so he could continue presenting his findings.

Finally, the leader clapped loudly. The group silenced instantly and turned to face him. He nodded to Hannes to continue.

"Oh…uh…so, when she built her online presence, she shared both her first and her last name. Vickie Hewitt."

Gabriel scowled. "Hewitt… Hewitt… that is not a vampire name. Are you sure this is the girl?"

"Yes, sir. It is very possible—in fact, likely—that she changed her name or entire identity. Vampires as a race were always crafty."

The leader nodded solemnly. "It has been our greatest fear. The craftiness of vampires was well documented. It is why the Sang Crusade came to be. The Circle needed an orchestrated attack on vampires to overwhelm them and overcome their fiendish intelligence. You believe, then, that she changed her identity."

"Yes, sir. She is listed online as 'Vicki Hewitt' from Milwaukee. This is her. I am sure of it. I continued to dig and I found records of sporting events she has participated in."

A few members of the Circle groaned. One of them stepped forward. "We are basing this all on sports records and online profiles? Our ancestors would be ashamed of us for going down this path."

Hannes grew anxious with frustration. "The only

Vickie Hewitt in Milwaukee has run races for Clear Lake High School. This is independent, official verification that she exists. Only last week, she completed a race. Look, this even has her picture."

He lifted a printout of the student photo that Craig had taken of Vickie. The Circle fell silent and stared at the image as they questioned whether this was a rebirth of the vampire race in the twenty-first century.

A few members challenged the idea openly.

"She's so young."

"That doesn't look like an evil threat."

"That's a teenager."

Gabriel raised his hand to silence them. "Members of the Slayer Circle, this girl's age does not concern me. If she is a vampire, she would be several hundred years old, at least. This would not be a teenage girl in that case. Regardless, if she is a vampire, she must die. Teenage threats grow up to be adult problems." He turned to Hannes. "Do you believe, in your heart of hearts, that your information is accurate?"

"Yes, sir."

"Would you be willing to gamble your life on that fact?"

Hannes swallowed hard and stared at the photos and records in his hands. "Yes, sir. I would."

"Very well." The leader took the photo from his hands and raised it above his head. "This is the future of the vampire race. She carries in her veins the blood of those who came before her and terrorized the world. It is our holy duty to exterminate this race once again and restore peace to this world. On this night, the Slayer Circle declares a new mission, one we will see through to the bitter end. If we do not fulfill the destiny laid out before us by our forefathers, we will bring shame to our ancestors and evil will overtake the world."

He stepped aside for a moment and returned to the circle with a long black sheath. With almost tender care, he slipped it off to reveal a long, sharp sword. Its metal reflected the candlelight in the darkness.

Gabriel raised it over his head with both hands and stared at it. The group followed his fixed gaze.

"This is the sword that christened the Sang Crusade generations ago. This weapon of holy destruction once bore the blood of Dominik, the bloodthirsty demon who robbed the world of so many lives. Our forefather, Konstantin Adler, wielded this sword with fury and right-eous rage. It is not only a symbol of the war that was fought in the name of honor and peace but also a valuable tool used to protect us and those we love. Tonight, we bring this sword back to life to once again serve as the protector. It will cut Vickie Hewitt down and eliminate the vampire race once again. The order has been declared."

"Sir," Hannes replied, "who will go to execute the order?"

He lowered the sword. "I will assemble the Soldiers of the Circle to go to America and put an end to this resurgence before it begins. The Soldiers will be led by myself and you, Hannes. Noah will also join us. Together, we will put a stop to this problem before it gets out of hand."

The old man who previously had the vision about Vickie stepped forward and faced Gabriel. "You do not know what you are getting yourself into."

"My friend," he said, "this is a war. It is difficult but we cannot back down. What would those who came before us think?"

"You don't understand. There is another."

They all looked at each other with concern. "What do you mean?"

"When you go to search out and exterminate the vampire, you will come into contact with another."

"Another vampire?" Hannes asked. "I did not find any evidence of another vampire anywhere in the world. She is the only one."

The old man shook his head sadly. "No, she is the last vampire. But there is another that is with her—something worse than a mere vampire. The blind spot of the Circle."

CHAPTER SIXTEEN

The hum of the mail truck launched Craig to his feet.

For a former journalist used to working in the "bullpen" of other reporters at an office, surrounded by activity, spending his hours making phone calls and badgering people for exclusives, working from home posed a challenge.

While he definitely enjoyed the freedom of his time and efforts, he wasn't prepared for how lonely an endeavor entrepreneurship could be.

He walked through the house and stepped outside his front door. *How pathetic is it that I am this excited over running out to collect the mail? I guess this is my first breath of fresh air all day. Sad.*

Once he reached the mailbox, he waved at the carrier who stuffed envelopes and flyers into their neighbor's mailbox before he speeded off on his route. *And that's the most human interaction I'll have today. Geez, maybe I should think about going to Target or something simply to be around other human beings for a while.*

With a handful of envelopes and other assorted papers, he strolled up the driveway and paused at the recycling container to sort the mail on the lid. *Bill. Bill. Ad. Flyer. Bill. Card. Bill. Flyer. Bill.* He picked up those he wanted to keep and slid the rest of the junk mail under the lid of the bin, then walked inside.

I might as well go through the bills now. It wouldn't hurt to mix the routine up a little. He tossed the pile of envelopes on the kitchen table, poured himself a glass of apple juice from the fridge, and took the checkbook out of the desk drawer.

Once seated, he sighed and resigned himself to the unpleasant task at hand. "Let's see the damage."

One by one, he tore each envelope open and added the bills to a low stack of papers beside him. He winced as he studied a few of them. *I don't remember the last time the energy bill was that high. Is this really our cell phone total? I need to talk to Alexis about how much data she uses. Boy, I wish I had thought about budgeting for two kids to go to high school. Tuition is out of control.*

He jotted down the numbers in the checkbook as he wrote out checks for each of them. Even though he ran his business online now, he preferred writing checks for the bills whenever possible. "It's easier to control your spending when it's inconvenient to do so," he often told his daughter. "Online bill pay lets you pay for stuff without thinking about it. I have to write the amount twice on a check, which makes it more real for me."

Once he reached the bottom of the stack and all the return envelopes were sealed with payments in them, he stared at the balance in the checkbook. *Is there a decimal out of place? Good grief. We'll have to choose between putting gas in the car or buying groceries this week.*

Craig tapped his pen nervously on the table as he tried to think of ways in which he could cover the bills and pay for the necessities. *I wonder how much I can get if I sold my kidney? I used to donate plasma in college for beer money. How many times a week can I do that?*

But while ridiculous ideas swirled in his head, he was merely distracting himself from the reality of his situation. He needed advertising money.

Because the advertiser had bailed on his podcast, he now only had half the income he normally received.

Frustrated with their financial situation, he yanked a notebook out of his desk and plopped it down on the table in front of him. *When you don't know what to do, start writing.*

To him, writing was a form of therapy. Whenever he felt overwhelmed with grief, he wrote his thoughts down. If he didn't know what to do next, he wrote all his options down. If he struggled with a decision, he'd note all the pros and cons.

He never kept the notes he wrote. Merely writing them got the ideas out of his head to where he could work with them on paper. This process became a valuable and effective tool for him—especially since professional therapy was so expensive.

Craig flipped the notebook open and began writing a stream of consciousness to empty his brain and lock himself in on a path to follow.

I really hate the fact that I can't pay my bills. What kind of a father can't provide for his family? It's driving me crazy. I always dreamed of being the breadwinner. Getting fired really hurt me. Okay, so how do I solve a problem like advertisers pulling out? Easy—get a bigger audience, right? If you have more people listening to every episode, you will attract more advertisers. Not only that, you'll also attract more money from those advertisers. You can raise your rates. That's what we need here. Perfect. You have an idea. Now, what can we change to? What is the problem? The Truth About... is still a great idea because it's easy to pivot to something else. That's why you chose it. We can wrap up Season two's cancer series. You need to do that anyway. It's time to move forward, and each episode is a little more painful than the last. It's not as therapeutic as you thought it would be.

He leaned back in his chair for a moment, closed his eyes, and scanned his thoughts in the vague hope that somewhere in their clutter, he might find a great idea for a new season of his podcast. His eyes snapped open and he leaned forward and scribbled quickly.

The Truth About... Blended Families (?)

Later that afternoon, Alexis walked in the door. After she'd dropped her bag in her room, she helped herself to a quick snack in the kitchen and sat on the couch in the living room.

"Hey, kid."

"Hey, Dad. How was your day?"

"Can't complain. How about yours?"

She shrugged like all teenagers do when fathers ask that question. "It was fine."

"Listen, I want to ask you about something—see if this sounds like a good idea to you."

She shoved a handful of potato chips in her mouth. "Let's hear it."

Her father raised his hands as if he were presenting a title on a marquee for her to see. "*The Truth About... Blended Families.*"

Alexis closed one eye. "Go on."

"I need to build a bigger audience for the podcast. Season two simply hasn't landed like I thought it would."

She looked confused. "I thought you were doing well."

"We're doing okay. But for us to grow—and for me to be able to pay all the bills in this house—the audience has to be bigger."

"You want to use to get a bigger audience?" She was not terribly impressed with the idea. In fact, the more she thought about it, the angrier she got. "Dad, this is kinda the opposite of what we want, isn't it? We're supposed to help make life feel normal for Vickie. That's the plan, right? Normal families don't air their dirty laundry online. And it's not only Vickie, it's us too! We don't know what normal looks like."

God bless your bleeding heart. Your mother gave that to you. "That's why I think it's important to do it in the first place. Think about it. There are families everywhere exactly like us. They are a mix of people from different backgrounds. Some families are run by single parents. There are all kinds of issues that come up with blended families—or families that undergo major life changes. Maybe we call it The Changing Family instead of Blended Families."

Alexis folded the bag of chips over and set it down on the floor next to the couch, stretched out with her head on a pillow, and stared at the ceiling. "It makes me feel weird, Dad. I don't know."

"Well, can you deal with a little weirdness?" He tried to

keep his composure, but it was hard to not sound desperate. "We'll not make it very far unless I come up with something. This podcast can work. I know it can. I simply need a better hook. Apparently, 'Former Journalist for the Milwaukee Journal-Sentinel' isn't enough of an attraction."

She chuckled. *You can't resist making a little joke, can you, Dad?* "What if everyone from school catches on? Now, we're drawing attention to ourselves. I don't want that. I know Vickie doesn't."

"We can make this up as we move forward with the idea. I'll protect you both in all of it somehow—code names or something. It could be good for all of us. Like therapy, except without the two-hundred-and fifty-dollars-an-hour price tag. It could be a lot of fun."

"What would we talk about, then?"

He put his hands on his hips. "Off the top of my head, the difference in cultures between Austria and America and how that impacts our family life, how we navigate the sudden loss of Mom, compare our story to blended and changing families in pop culture like The Brady Bunch or Modern Family. We're like the real-world version of Modern Family. See, there are many different ways we can take it and have fun with it."

She still didn't like the idea but she also knew it was a good one—and she wanted to help her dad. At the same time, she didn't want to risk negatively affecting Vickie. "I want her to be normal, Dad."

He walked over and sat on the couch beside her. "Of course. And she is normal. She's fitting in. People love her. But we both know we're not an average family anymore. And there are many people out there who might not have vampires in their family, but they are dealing with the roller coaster ride we're on, too. This could be a great way to help them, right?"

Alexis sat up and looked him squarely in the eye. "How bad is our financial situation?"

Craig exhaled slowly as he tried to think of a way to phrase it. He came from a family that did not talk openly about money with the kids, so he didn't want to put his financial burdens on his daughter. He honestly felt she had enough of her own issues to deal with.

"Let's put it this way…if I can't grow my audience, we'll have to talk about you getting a job to contribute to the monthly bills."

She gritted her teeth. "We'll talk to Vickie about getting me and her on the podcast."

He gave her a playful jab on her shoulder and stood. "Yep, that's what I thought. You know, I really should lead off conversations like that. It would save me time. 'Hey, honey, if you go to that concert on Friday night, you'll probably have to get a job and contribute to the monthly bills.'"

The girl smirked. "That doesn't even make sense, Dad."

He chuckled as he walked down the hall to his bedroom. "It doesn't have to make sense as long as it works."

CHAPTER SEVENTEEN

Vickie sat up in her bed that Saturday morning and noticed the sunshine peeking through the blinds covering her window.

Please be nice out. Come on, sunshine.

She peered around the blinds and saw nothing but blue sky. *Perfect.*

It took only a moment to slip on a pair of black jogging pants and a baggy gray hoodie with *CLEAR LAKE HIGH* embroidered across the front. Quietly, she turned the doorknob and stepped into the hall.

When the door closed behind her with a faint click, she listened intently toward the back bedrooms to be sure there was no activity from either of them. *Both are still sleeping. Good. They'd better be at six a.m. on a Saturday.*

The vampire tiptoed into the kitchen, found a post-it note, and scrawled, *Out for breakfast, back soon – V,* on it. Then, she walked to the side door, pulled her shoes on, and unlocked it.

She paused for a second to admire the new replacement

door. The old wooden one that had been a part of the house for twenty-five years had been removed after she'd splintered it. In its place was a modern, solid door made from steel-reinforced composite materials.

The old wood door had creaked loudly when you opened it, but the replacement was whisper-quiet, which allowed her to sneak out unnoticed.

The rush of freedom followed on the tail of the first big gust of wind. It was a chilly morning, but the sunshine made it tolerable for her. She shoved her hands into the front pockets of her hoodie to keep warm and turned left at the end of the driveway.

While Vickie had operated in the world of high school on her own, she needed to know that she could be a member of society in general by herself. That was why she now ventured down the street to eat breakfast all alone in public.

It also gave her time to reflect.

Alexis has been great, but I can't have her holding my hand all the time. I have to learn how to do these things myself. I want to be able to go out on dates with Eric and not have Alexis there. And especially not Will. Ugh, don't think about Will right now, Vickie. You can't risk your teeth poking out here.

She still didn't know her directions particularly well, but she remembered where the pharmacy store was where they witnessed the robbery. Next door to that was a fast-food restaurant that served breakfast.

Just walk there, have a breakfast sandwich of some kind and a cup of juice, and come home. It couldn't be easier. You can do this.

Vickie had spent so much time focused on which direction she had to go in and how to not get lost that she hadn't really paid attention to the neighborhood she was in.

As she walked along the street, the blight of the neighborhood struck her. Fast food wrappers lined the streets alongside old, cracked liquor bottles. In one yard, a rusted charcoal grill rested on its side. Everywhere she looked, she saw garbage.

More than a few houses had bedsheets hung as curtains. Some windows were broken or completely removed. Overgrown grass matted in places where wandering dogs simply did their business anywhere they pleased.

Is this really how people live around here? This is so depressing.

She reached an intersection and stood patiently on the curb as she waited for the crosswalk light to switch. To her confusion, one guy was already walking across even though the signal hadn't changed yet. Another older woman walked confidently in a diagonal pattern through the entire intersection, not wanting to cross twice.

Doesn't anyone follow the rules around here?

Drivers raced through red lights. Even at six a.m., loud music pumped from aftermarket speakers and the bass seemed to rattle the ground she stood on.

Vickie crossed the street quickly when the signal turned, and she paused in front of the pharmacy. *I wonder if they caught that guy. I sure hope so. No one should get away with something like that.*

She turned to look at the other side of the street. A middle-aged man in a dirty jacket and stained tan pants watched her from the bus stop. At first, she ignored him and simply assumed that their eyes had met in passing.

But every time she looked back, he continued to stare at her, wide-eyed, and made no effort to hide. His long black hair was brushed back, and the gray beard that bushed around his chin made the experience feel sleazier for her.

Her instinct told her to confront him. If he gave her any trouble, she could snap his arm and be on her way. But Alexis' voice echoed in her head. *That's not how we do things here.*

The vampire accepted the reminder and she continued up the road to the restaurant. The golden arches reminded her of when she saw the restaurant in Salzburg in her first drive around town after waking up. *It's amazing how time flies. Now, I'm an American high school student in the twenty-first century.*

With a self-satisfied smile, she walked into the restaurant. The smell of breakfast sausage teased her nose and made her mouth water.

The establishment was relatively empty. Only a few people stood in line—some elderly couples and a few sleepy-eyed construction workers.

When it was her turn at the counter, a wave of excitement rushed through her. Although it was something as simple as ordering food, she didn't have a safety net with her.

She successfully ordered a bacon, egg, and cheese bagel with an apple juice and handed over the five-dollar bill she had in her pocket. After she'd taken her change, she stepped aside to wait for her order.

Vickie tucked her hair behind her ears and smiled. *This isn't so bad. I'm doing it.*

Once her order was ready, she took her tray and moved

to a table facing the window so she could enjoy the view—
what there was of it—as she ate.

The bagel was delicious and the apple juice was refreshing. But, as she ate, she couldn't shake the nagging feeling
that she was being watched.

Her senses didn't spiral out of control, but they did
heighten. *The old couple number one keeps staring at me, likely
wondering what I'm doing out so early in the morning. Old
couple number two has glanced over here three times, probably
wondering why I'm out by myself. And the two construction
workers are looking at me in a very different fashion, which
really grosses me out.*

That last one made her eat a little more quickly. While
she didn't feel like she was in any immediate danger, she
also wasn't interested in sticking around anyone who made
her uncomfortable—especially since this was her first time
out by herself.

She devoured the rest of her bagel, chugged the apple
juice, and managed to stifle a rather loud burp. *Old couple
number one are now judging me for not being very ladylike.*

When she left the restaurant, Vickie noticed more
people were out. At a gas station on the corner, two guys
stood beside a car while one pumped gas. Both watched
her speculatively while she walked past.

The bearded man had gone, but beyond the bus stop
stood an apartment building. Out on the balcony, a
young man puffed on a cigarette while he looked down
at her.

I need to get out of here. I need to get home. This is enough.

She began to power-walk, focused on the need to get
home, but grew more and more anxious. *You don't know*

what kind of danger you're in. Who cares what these people think? Do what you need to do to get home.

The vampire inhaled sharply, glanced furtively around her, then tapped into her super-speed and rocketed home. She stopped in the middle of the driveway and immediately saw Alexis stare at her from the living room window with her palms in the air and her mouth hanging open.

Vickie smiled and waved, then walked into the house.

"Are you kidding me?" the other girl said immediately.

"What?"

"Let's start with you going out unannounced in this neighborhood." She folded her arms, fuming with anger.

"I wanted to get breakfast and thought that was an easy task to do on my own. What's the big deal?"

"Vickie, the big deal is you're not an adult in this era. You're only fourteen. Fourteen-year-old girls don't go out by themselves in this neighborhood. It doesn't matter the time of day. There are way too many weirdos around here."

"Well, you're right about that."

"And the speed?" Alexis couldn't believe she had to talk about this again. "What's with using your powers in broad daylight like this? Someone could easily call the cops."

"I had to get home and I didn't like my surroundings. I simply speeded up the process. I know people might be freaking out right now—although I don't think anyone saw me—but they don't know where I live or who I am. So it's okay. I got home safely."

"I'm trying really hard to help you stay in your lane," her sister said earnestly. "I'm not trying to hurt or frustrate you. I'm helping you. You're not quite ready to go out everywhere by yourself. Please work with me on this. I can't help if you sneak out of the house." For a moment, she felt like a mother.

Vickie sighed. "I'm only trying to have some freedom. I want to be able to move around when I want to."

"You will. You merely have to be a little older for that to happen. We're not in that place yet. Hey, I'm not either. We have to be annoyed and miserable together for a while. It'll be worth it, I promise."

She nodded and sat on the couch beside her. "Breakfast was good, though."

Alexis giggled. "I'm glad it was worth it for you. And for crying out loud, stop using your powers in front of people. I'm begging you. I don't know how many ways I can cover that up for you."

The vampire tapped her on the knee. "I'm trying my best. Some days are harder than others."

"Hey, if I had super-powers, I'd probably use them all the time too."

CHAPTER EIGHTEEN

If Craig's worst nightmare was driving his daughters and their boyfriends to the Homecoming Dance, hosting a visit with the boys at his house was his second worst nightmare.

The girls decided to invite their boys for a Saturday night hangout. They were in the basement, getting ready.

"So is this a double date, then?" Vickie asked while they pulled the green vinyl cover off the pool table and folded it.

"Mmmm, not really." Alexis took the folded cover and slipped it under the table. "A date is technically when you go somewhere. Since we're only hanging out here, it's a little less pressure. I thought it would be good for you. Besides, we want Dad to see that they're great guys."

She nodded. "Of course, he should know who his daughters are marrying, right?"

"Whoa, whoa, whoa." The other girl held her hands up. "Aren't you forgetting something?"

Vickie covered her face with her hand. "Oh, that's right.

I'm sorry. Marriage at this age was a thing in my past life. This isn't about getting married."

"Not in high school, it isn't. And it's a good thing you had that slip-up now and not when the guys are here." She turned on the light above the dart board.

The vampire looked around the basement. The couches surrounded a nice TV, the pool table, dart board, and air hockey table, and a dry bar stood in the corner, stocked with liquor.

"Are all American homes like this?"

"What do you mean?" Alexis opened the fridge behind the bar to grab a soda.

"In my castle, they turned it into a rex room."

"That's rec room, not rex room."

She giggled. "Oh, right. Anyway, this basement looks really similar to that one. Is that a thing?"

"It depends on the house. I don't think very many houses are as stocked as ours is, though." Alexis smiled when she thought of the parties her family used to throw. "We were the house that hosted parties often. Big family get-togethers, summer shindigs, Super Bowl parties. There was always a reason to have everyone over. My parents loved doing that."

This confused Vickie. "I've been here for a few months now and we haven't had one party."

"Yeah, well, my dad hasn't been in much of a partying mood in recent months. When you lose your wife and your job at the same time, you tend to lose the partying spirit. And I know he had more fun planning those things with my mom. Now come on, let me give you a crash course in some of these games quickly before the guys get here."

Upstairs, the doorbell rang. Craig slung the dish towel over his shoulder and walked from the sink to the side door. He opened it, and Eric stood before him with a slightly nervous smile.

"Hi, Mr. Watson."

"Eric." He nodded to him and let him in the house.

The boy had always gotten along well with him. He could tell that Eric was a bright, innocent kid who was loyal to his friends and respected the people around him. But he also showed no interest in dating his daughter. Now that he was dating Vickie—practically a daughter of Craig's now—the dynamic had shifted.

Eric became Just Another High School Boy, and Craig worried that he only had one thing on his mind.

"Another big win for the Pack last week," Eric said awkwardly in an attempt to strike up a conversation. "How do you think they'll do against the Bears tomorrow night?"

"They'll do fine, Eric." He turned his back to him while he washed dishes. "The Packers have the Bears' number every year."

"Ha-ha, you got that right." The boy nodded but could feel the tension in the air. "Are the girls downstairs?"

Craig turned and gave him a stern look. "Yep. And that door stays open tonight, by the way."

"Oh, of course. Yes, sir." Eric slunk down the stairs to greet the girls.

Not long after that, the doorbell rang again. *All right, let's try to be nice here. Your daughter likes him, and that's what matters right now.*

He opened the door, and Will looked up at him with that expressionless face he found so disconcerting. "Sir."

"Will."

The new arrival simply walked in, heard the voices coming from the basement, and immediately went down the stairs.

Oh, I do not like this kid at all. He shook his head in disappointment. *That guy gives me such a bad vibe.*

Craig did his best to avoid eavesdropping, but like most parents, he felt it was his duty to make sure that everything was good and proper down in the basement.

To his relief, it mostly sounded like innocent fun. The group moved from pool table to air hockey to darts as they laughed and cracked jokes as much as possible.

When it came time for them to watch a movie, it became much quieter down there. He kept trying to shake his nagging concerns but would somehow constantly return to the top of the stairs. *They're watching a movie. Of course they'll be quiet. They're trying to hear the movie. I hope.*

The girls had turned the lights off down there, so he saw that as his ticket. He marched down the stairs and flipped the light switch on. To his relief, the kids sat innocently on the couch, watching the movie.

"Do you mind, Dad?"

"Just…keep the light on, okay? Thanks."

Frustrated, he returned upstairs and wandered into the living room. *You raised her right. She's a good influence on Vickie. Eric is a good guy. If Will tried anything, Alexis wouldn't stand for it. Eric would defend her. And Vickie could literally kill him within seconds. You're fine. They're fine. Now let them be. Let them have a good time together.*

That was easier said than done. He spent the evening watching sitcoms on TV and didn't actually recall a single one. Despite every effort, he couldn't shake the nagging feeling that some kind of misbehavior was happening in the basement.

After they left at the end of the night, Craig allowed himself to go to bed.

The next morning, over breakfast, he wanted to talk to them about the relationships they were enjoying.

He stuck a mouthful of scrambled eggs on the end of his fork. "So, girls, did you have fun last night?"

"Yeah, we did, Dad."

"Good."

Another awkward pause followed while everyone ate.

"Okay, I want to talk to you about something." They put their forks down and looked at him to see where he was going with the conversation. "So, you both are dating boys these days, and I'm really happy for you. I think you both are plenty old enough and responsible enough to handle it."

Alexis nodded. "Thanks, Dad." *And now, the other shoe will drop.*

Her father took a deep breath. "We need to talk about high school boys. Girls, high school boys are really only interested in one thing—"

"Oh, no." Alexis interrupted. "Please, Dad, don't do this."

"I'm only trying to—"

"No. Dad. Seriously. We're fine. We won't do anything."

He put his hand on the table. "Lex, it's not that I don't trust you. I'm your father, and this is part of being a father to teenage girls. We have to talk about this kind of thing openly."

His daughter's face flushed. "Dad, we know what to do

and what not to do, okay? Don't be embarrassing. I'll lose my appetite here."

Craig breathed slowly, then turned to Vickie, who had remained silent the entire time. "Do you know what I'm talking about?"

"I think so." Her voice was timid and shy. Being an old-fashioned girl, she came from a time when that wasn't discussed.

"Okay then, let me pivot this a little."

"Dad, please don't be gross. I'm begging you."

"I won't be gross. I promise. Here's the second half of that talk, since you appear to be confident enough in your understanding of the first half of it. I am sure that you were much more comfortable talking with your mom about boys and your female issues and anything else that came to mind. Problems with friends, whatever. You and Mom were tight about that stuff, right?"

Alexis nodded. She could talk to her mom about anything, and she missed that.

"No matter what it is, if either of you is in trouble, or struggling with something, or afraid of something, or something happened that was bad, or embarrassing, or whatever it could possibly be...I want you to know that you can always talk to me."

"What if it's something really bad?" Alexis asked with a devilish smirk.

"Give me an example."

"Let's say I tell you I'm hanging out with Jess and Jamie, but I actually go to Will's house because his parents are out of town."

Vickie's stomach twisted. *Like that would ever happen.*

You'd have to get him to say more than three words to find out where he lived.

Her father steadied himself and worked hard not to overreact. "Sweetheart, if that happened and you found yourself in a bad situation, I would still be willing and able to help you out if you needed it." He paused. "That didn't happen though, right?"

She laughed. "Dad, come on. You can trust me. I promise."

They finished breakfast, and the girls excused themselves while Craig cleaned up. As he lowered the plates into the sink, he looked out the window and thought of his wife.

You had to leave before she started dating, didn't you? This is some kind of retribution for something I did. It has to be. You're getting back at me for some mistake or oversight. Did I forget our anniversary or something?

He smiled and turned the faucet on to rinse the plates off. *This sure would be so much easier if you were here to help me. You were always better at covering the serious stuff with her. I'm more of the joke guy, which I know you hated. Still, having a teammate on this stuff would have been nice.*

CHAPTER NINETEEN

"Dad? What are you doing here?"

Craig greeted his daughter at her locker with a goofy smile. "I'm a student here now—surprise. I'm in all your classes. I can't wait to embarrass you by passing around baby pictures of you in the bathtub."

She returned her attention to her locker and tried to hide a smile. Alexis knew it was a dumb joke and didn't want to encourage more of them, although she knew she couldn't stop him. "Seriously, though, why are you here? Are you coming to pick me up? Is everything okay?"

"Relax. I am going to take you home since I'm here already, but Vickie's coach called and said he wanted to meet with me."

The girl stopped and gave him a confused look. "About what?"

"Beats me." He stuck his hands in his pockets and looked down the hallway. "I guess it's serious, otherwise he would've told me on the phone, wouldn't he?"

Uh oh. Did Vickie let her guard down again? Did she hurt someone and not tell me? "Can I come with you?"

Her father shrugged. "You can. I don't know if he'll allow you in there. You might want to wait. Hey, Vickie."

The vampire greeted him with confused enthusiasm. He explained why he was there and told her to come along too.

When they reached Coach Lueck's classroom, he greeted all three of them warmly. "Girls, would you mind waiting outside for a few minutes while I talk with your dad? Or…uh, uncle? Whatever?"

They hung out in the hallway while Coach closed the door and offered Craig a seat.

"So, is there something wrong with Vickie? Did she do something bad? I don't really know what bad behavior is on the cross country team."

Coach Lueck laughed. "No, no, no, don't worry about that. Vickie is an absolute sweetheart. She's great, she runs hard, and she has a real knack for the sport."

He's buttering me up to lower the boom. "So what's the problem?"

The coach hesitated with a smile on his face. "This is silly. I have been asked by some officials from another school to investigate an issue that a runner had with Vickie out on the course."

"Uh oh. Did she hurt someone?" *That blasted super-strength. She can't go anywhere with that.*

"No, not at all. They just…um, one of the girls claims that Vickie has super-speed."

Play dumb. Play as dumb as you can possibly play. Come on, you used to act in high school. Tap into that. "What do you mean by super-speed?"

Coach Lueck winced. "I honestly don't know. She says that they were in a stretch of the race where things were getting a little…you know, dicey, competitive—chippy! That's the word I'm looking for. And according to this runner, Vickie suddenly surged forward and disappeared in a flash."

It looks like he's talking nonsense. "Okay…so do hallucinations come up often during races?"

The man laughed. "No, I knew it was ridiculous. But they seem to think something happened back there that showed she had some unfair advantage."

"Is running faster than the other girls something you would call an unfair advantage, Coach?"

"No, sir. I merely promised them that I would look into it."

Craig pointed to the door. "Well, go ahead and talk to her about it. Bring the girls in here and see what they have to say."

Lueck got up from his desk, opened the door, and ushered the girls in.

"Am I in trouble? Did I do something wrong?" Vickie appeared concerned. "I really like being on the team so please don't kick me off."

"Oh, we're not kicking you off, Vickie. You're one of our strongest runners. No, you're fine. We merely had a complaint filed against you by another runner."

"Who?" Vickie started growing defensive, ready to argue against any accusations made against her.

"I can't say. They merely claimed that you had some

kind of super-speed ability that you tapped into and over-took everyone. You know, the more I say it out loud, the more ridiculous it sounds." He laughed.

"Does any of that sound familiar?" Craig asked Vickie. "Did you have trouble with any runners out on the course during the meet?"

"Yes, I did have trouble." She pulled up her pant leg to show the bandages wrapped around her calf. "One girl spent the whole stretch kicking me whenever I got closer to her."

"Gosh, I don't know why anyone would make that up. This is so strange," the coach muttered.

"Maybe she wanted to get in front of it," Alexis suggested. "Sometimes, you accuse someone else before they can accuse you, right?"

He nodded slowly. "That makes sense."

Craig leaned back in his chair, his hands on his head. "Do you have any daughters, sir?" Lueck shook his head. "They have fairly wild imaginations. But what makes this even more complicated is that they often believe whatever it is they are saying that might not even be connected to reality."

"Really?"

"Oh yeah. If a girl doesn't like someone, they will convince themselves of all sorts of evil activity. I think, based on how you've presented this, the girl was being outrun by Vickie, even in the face of leg wounds, and she got mad at her and decided she didn't deserve to beat her. While she's focused on that, Vickie ran past her and simply moved on with her life without her noticing." *That's not bad. Good quick thinking on your feet.*

"Well, Vickie, I owe you an apology. I'm sorry for having to raise this and make you freak out a little. You're doing great, seriously. You all should be very proud."

"We are."

"You're a hard runner, and you're tough, as far as I can see. I love to see that on my team."

As they all stood to leave, Coach looked at Vickie one more time with a wink and said, "And no speeding."

Outside the classroom, however, there was no such relief. The second they got into the car, Craig turned to face the vampire in the back seat.

"You used your speed powers in a race? Are you crazy? How many other runners saw you and didn't say anything?"

She shrugged. "I didn't do it for fun or to win the race. I did it because this girl was carving my legs up."

He rubbed his temples. "I understand that, and I'm sorry you had to go through it. But that's life. Sometimes, it sucks and sometimes, it's uncomfortable. And those of us who don't have magical powers simply have to deal with it."

Alexis nodded as she added, "Vickie, we are doing everything in our power to keep your identity under wraps and away from the public. You've slipped up a lot lately, and it's really making us worry."

She remained quiet. *I don't know why they're making such a big deal out of this. I'll be fine.*

"Vickie, if you don't keep this a secret, we can't promise that you'll be safe." Craig twisted all the way around in the driver's seat to be sure he would get the point across. "We keep you in something of a bubble. When you go out of that bubble—and you will someday—you don't have our protection anymore. The government could come in here and whisk you off to some lab where they run experiments on you. Or some sleazeball will try to make you an oddity that people pay money to see—the Bearded Lady, the Monkey Boy, and the Vampire Girl, or something."

"We're not trying to control you," Alexis assured her. "We're only trying to find a way to protect you so you can avoid some of those more major consequences. And that starts with not using your powers in public."

"We've said that many times, Vickie. I need assurance that this is getting through to you because we are one slip-up away from losing you forever. Keep a tight lid on that stuff. Deal with the limitations of being human. You'll be surprised how great it is when you remove that burden from yourself."

Vickie sighed. She knew what they were saying but at the same time, she had powers she wanted to use. Regularly. And Craig hadn't built anything to replace his gym setup that she destroyed. She needed an outlet for that energy, both mental and physical.

"I wanted to talk to you about something, Vickie." Craig needed to get moving on his podcast. "We've talked about ways to improve my podcast, and I thought of making you and Alexis permanent guests. We can talk about the struggles of you coming to America and how we cope together as a family. I don't know if Alexis brought it up yet, but it's something I've been kicking around. We can hash out all the details later. For now, keep it in the back of your mind."

Later that evening, Vickie and Alexis sat at the kitchen table and sketched out ideas for car designs. A small cardboard box rested on the table beside them, along with a few coat hangers.

"This is really frustrating." Alexis shook her head while they stared at the box. "How do we turn this thing into a car?"

"That's not even half of it. How do we turn it into a car that will beat Megan's?" The vampire grew more annoyed by the minute. "This thing has to travel really far, and it doesn't even have wheels yet."

"One thing at a time." Her sister placed her hand on the table. "Let's get this built, then we can figure out how to make it better."

As they sat in silent concentration, a squeaking noise came from the living room.

Vickie looked at Alexis, who didn't react to it. *Maybe I'm hearing things.* But the squeaking continued. *I definitely am hearing that.* "What is that sound?"

"What sound?"

"The squeaking. You don't hear that? It's driving me crazy."

"Oh. That's my dad." Alexis laughed. "He's eating cheese curds. Dad. Come in here."

Her father strolled into the room carrying a small plastic bag filled with little orange nuggets of cheese. He popped one in his mouth. "What's up, girls?" Every time he bit down, his mouth squeaked.

"Vickie doesn't know what cheese curds are."

He held the bag out in front of her. "Oh, man, are you

missing out. These are my favorite snack. I eat them all the time. I'm surprised you haven't noticed. Try one."

Reluctantly, she complied and selected one of the nuggets. She bit it, and it squeaked loudly.

Craig smiled. "That sound means you have a good one. Cheese curds are a staple here in Wisconsin. You won't find them in many other places. We're known for them."

She chewed on the squeaky cheese. The saltiness combined with the cheesy flavor was incredibly satisfying. "These are delicious."

"Of course they are. But if you want some, you'll have to get your own when we go shopping next."

Alexis shook her head and grinned. "Dad doesn't share his curds. He's really particular about that."

"That first one was a bonus, Vickie. You should feel honored I was even willing to give that one up. What are you girls working on?"

Vickie pointed to the notebook as she chewed the rest of her curd. "I need to build a car. We'll use this box as the body, but we don't really know what to use for wheels."

"I thought maybe we could poke holes in some tennis balls or something?" *I'm really not good at this. I shouldn't be helping.*

Craig looked at the design and thought for a moment. *What would be big and round but flat?* He snapped his fingers. "I have an idea," he muttered and disappeared down the hallway.

The girls heard him clunking around in his bedroom closet. He soon emerged with a large black case with a zipper on it. Craig opened it to reveal a binder full of CDs.

"What are these?" Vickie asked.

"These are how old people listened to music before everyone subscribed to every song ever online. You can use them to build wheels. Since we got that family Spotify subscription, I don't really need them anymore."

Alexis laughed as she paged through the many discs. "I haven't even heard of some of these people. Pearl Jam? Nirvana? The Smashing Pumpkins?"

"You laugh, but those bands were major back when I was a teenager. Go ahead and use as many as you want."

Vickie slipped one of the CDs out of the case and looked at the label. "What's a Weezer?"

"Don't worry about it." Her sister waved her hand impatiently. "These will actually make awesome wheels. They're perfect."

The girls piled up a few CDs and played around with them to see how they could make them work on the car.

CHAPTER TWENTY

Vickie's legs tangled in the blankets on her bed as she tossed and turned that night. She sat up, fluffed her pillow, and laid back down again but couldn't get comfortable.

Her stomach tightened again, and it became so uncomfortable that she knew there was no way she could fall asleep.

With a frustrated sigh, she yanked the covers off her bed and stood in the pitch-black room. Even standing straight proved to be a struggle. The tightness was almost too much to bear.

I can't sleep because my body is telling me to be a vampire. But I can't be a vampire or I'll get in trouble. Was coming here a mistake? Am I doomed to a life of sleepless nights now? Is this what I will have to deal with on a regular basis?

On the assumption that she could rid herself of the issue by embracing her powers once again, she changed into the faded white gown and snuck out of the house into the cold night.

But as she poised and prepared to run, she stopped.

This isn't right. This isn't the same thing. I'm not itching to be a vampire. This is danger. Something's wrong and it's getting worse.

With no obvious solution, she paced around the back yard and tried to shake the feeling in the pit of her stomach. Nothing seemed to bring any relief or enlightenment.

She looked at the sky. "You didn't prepare me. You saved me, but you didn't prepare me. I didn't know anything. You didn't teach me about what it means to be a vampire. You locked me up in that box and preserved my life, but you did nothing to preserve my legacy. I don't know who I am, what I am, or what any of this means."

When she realized she was shouting rather loudly, Vickie walked behind the shed and sank down until she sat in the dirt.

You kept me alive physically, but you didn't keep me alive mentally or emotionally.

She squeezed her eyes shut. *Come on. There has to be something. Anything. If you have to find it out yourself, fine. So, what is it?*

Briefly, her mind drifted to the talk Craig had attempted to give the girls the other night. *It had been awkward, but it was a father trying to teach his daughters something important about their bodies and their lives. My father and mother never taught me anything about my body or—*

The vampire felt as though someone had flipped a switch in her brain. Her mouth fell open. "My parents did try to teach me."

She crossed her legs and closed her eyes again as she

concentrated on pulling that thread in her mind. *What did they try to teach me? And when? Can I still remember it?*

Over and over, she repeated those questions to herself and attempted to force the memories through her mind. Soon, flashes of recall slid past her consciousness—playing with her siblings, helping her mother around the house, horsing around in the yard with her father.

Vickie smiled and opened her eyes. She stood in the foyer of the castle, only it was still four hundred years ago. She looked at her arms and legs and waved them around. They had a foggy appearance, but everything else she looked at was the same.

It seemed that she had woken up from a short nap centuries ago—like she always expected to.

"Hello?" Her voice bounced off the cavernous walls.

She walked into the library, stunned to see the much smaller group of books that she remembered. When she walked into the old, dark kitchen, her mother stood and stirred broth in a large cast iron pot over a fire.

Vickie's lip quivered. She reached out to hug her mother, but her arms passed right through her. "Mutter?" The woman didn't look up from her pot. "Mutter! It's me, Victoria. Your daughter."

To her further shock, her father walked through the doorway of the kitchen area along with a younger version of herself riding on his back.

The vampire's throat instantly tightened. Not only was it wonderful to see her father again, but she was taken aback by how different she herself looked.

No makeup. A clean gown. No product in her hair, merely straight and dark.

This is a memory. This is something that happened in the past. I can't talk to them because they're not really here. I'm not really here. This is all in my head.

Little Victoria walked across the kitchen and sat at the table to stare out the window. Her parents stood on either side of her, and her father leaned forward to speak to her.

"My little dear, you are getting older."

"I'm almost thirteen," Little Victoria shouted. Vickie smiled warmly at her former enthusiasm.

"That's right, my girl. But this also means you have to learn more about the world around you."

"Your father is right," her mother interjected. "There are people in this world who do not approve of you."

"Why not? What did I do?"

He placed his hand on his daughter's back. "Nothing, sweetheart. Nothing at all. You are wonderful in every way. But the world sees vampires differently. They do not approve of any of us—you, me, your mother, or your siblings."

"What do they want to do to us?"

The parents looked at each other and nodded. "They want to hurt us very badly."

Little Victoria covered her mouth in shock. "What do we do? How can we keep them from hurting us?"

Her father nodded calmly. "I promise you, they will never hurt you. Ever. I will make sure of that."

Vickie blinked through the tears. *That's one thing you followed through with, Father. You made sure no one would lay a hand on me. And they never did. I wish I could thank you right now for that.*

"But the beautiful thing, my dear child, is that we vampires have a built-in sense for danger."

"We do?"

"Yes, we do. When you are in danger, you will feel it right here." He touched her stomach with his index finger. "It will feel very tight. But it will tell you if there is danger nearby or coming that you should be aware of."

The girl frowned. "How will I know if someone is a danger to me or not, though? Can I do anything to keep it from happening?"

Her mother knelt beside her worried daughter and threw her arms around her neck. "Let's put it this way, dear daughter. There are a few bad people in this world. If they know you exist, they will come for you. If you feel that danger in your body, it means someone is coming for you."

"But don't be scared," her father hastened to add. "You have been blessed with many abilities that make you a far superior creature than anyone who might try to attack you for who you are."

Vickie stared at the three of them, then let her eyes wander. *I can't believe I'm standing in this house again. It truly feels like my home. And my parents! I don't think about how much I miss them.*

"I'm sorry," she shouted to them, although they couldn't hear her. "I'm sorry, Mutter and Vater. I'm not trying to hide or deny my vampire upbringing. I simply don't know what to do."

Her father continued talking to Little Victoria. "As you get older, your sense of danger will be a tool to protect you. Listen to it. If you feel it deep inside you, someone is coming. If you can attack, do so. If you need to hide, do that. But always listen to your gut."

Her mother nodded. "Always listen. Listen more than you talk. And that goes double for the voice inside you. Listen to that voice. Cherish it. Respect it. It will never steer you the wrong way."

Vickie nodded in agreement from across the room. She knew that listening to your gut was an important part of being a vampire. She merely hadn't realized how important it was.

With tears streaming down her cheeks, she tried one more time to throw her arms around her parents and hug them. Of course, she stepped forward and passed right through them. She took a step back and choked the words out, "Thank you." In the next instant, she opened her eyes in the present day.

The vampire wiped the tears from her cheeks and looked around at the night sky and the open field. *So, if I feel this way, it means that there is danger coming. It must have something to do with Will since I have had that feeling repeatedly around him. But what about the feeling I get here at home?*

She walked around the house to see if there were any other reasons why she would have this feeling. There were no physical threats.

Vickie stood in the driveway and scrutinized the area. *What is the cause of all this tightness and discomfort?*

Then she remembered her father's advice. She closed her eyes, placed her hands on her belly, and took a few deep breaths. They filled her with energy and allowed her to listen to what her gut was telling her.

Someone is coming. Someone big is coming and they are not

only a threat to you physically. They are adamant in their quest to rid the world of vampires. Their purpose is to eliminate lives.

The vampire opened her eyes and inhaled deeply. "It's the Circle. The Circle knows I am here and they will come for me."

Her gut shifted, and that told her she had identified what had bothered her.

But that is only the beginning. How will I find the Circle? How will they find me? If they do find me, will I have the chance to fight back? Or will they simply execute me on the spot? And what will happen to my family? Will they be executed as well, or are they expected to see this unfold and forget it ever happened?

She had tapped into a very powerful force. Now, she merely had to learn how to use it most effectively.

CHAPTER TWENTY-ONE

Alexis was the first to notice how quiet Vickie was the next morning.

The two girls sat at the kitchen table, eating breakfast. Normally, the vampire would fire off a few questions about the day or about something she hadn't seen before.

Initially, her sister waved it off. *She must be catching up. She's been here a while and is probably running out of questions.*

But after breakfast, she was still silent. Alexis caught her staring out the window on several occasions, deep in thought.

"Are you okay?" she asked finally.

"I'm fine." The vampire turned her gaze from the window. "Why?"

"You seem like something's bothering you. Is everything good with Eric?"

"Eric's good, yeah. No problems. He's great."

Another long pause followed.

"Ookay." Alexis figured the girl would open up at some

point. She didn't want to push her too far, too quickly. *Maybe she'll talk on her own later.*

Vickie sat on the couch in the living room and leafed through a magazine when the doorbell rang. The Watsons didn't get too many visitors, so the doorbell caught her attention. She straightened quickly, pushed off the couch, and pressed herself against the wall.

Her heart thudded a little as she leaned forward and tried to peek through the curtains and see who was at the door. *I can't be too careful. That could be anyone. Of course they would ring the doorbell. They wouldn't know that we never get visitors here.*

Alexis bounded into the room with a smile on her face. "What are you doing?"

She waved her hand frantically and then raised her finger to her lips. "Sssshhh!" she said quietly. "There's someone at the door."

"Yeah, I know." Her sister walked past her and unlocked the front door despite the whispered protests behind her.

There was no one there. Puzzled, she looked around, then down, and saw a large package on the step. She pumped her fist and pulled it into the house.

As she shut the door behind her and locked it, Vickie stepped away from the wall. "Who was it?" she asked suspiciously.

"No one. It was the UPS guy dropping this box off. They simply ring the doorbell and leave."

"Oh." *You're a little too jumpy. Rein it in before you hurt someone.* "So…what's in the box, then?"

"I'll show you in a minute. Come on."

The two girls returned to the kitchen, and Alexis set the

heavy box on the table. She sat and motioned for her companion to sit opposite her.

"Here's what we'll do. You'll tell me what's on your mind, and I'll show you what's in the box." *I'm tired of waiting around.*

"I…I don't know what you're talking about." She tried her best to look like she was fine, but her eyes told Alexis she was anything but.

"Come on, girl, I know you by now. There's something bothering you, and I want to know what it is."

"Why? Don't I get to have a little privacy? You talk about that all the time with your dad."

"Not when the person I'm living with is a vampire who can sense danger. You obviously know there's something going on and you're not telling me. 'Fess up, and I'll tell you what's in the box."

Vickie was cornered, and it annoyed her. She didn't want to divulge that trouble was brewing as it would worry the family. At the same time, she didn't want to keep it a secret from them either.

"All right, here it is. I had a vision last night."

"What kind of vision?"

"It was…kind of like a replay. I was back in my home and I saw myself as a child being talked to by my parents."

"Whoa." The girl's eyes widened. "So you got to see your parents again?"

"Kind of. They weren't alive, necessarily, but their shades were there. Apparently, when I was a little younger, they started to teach me about these feelings in the pit of my stomach."

"The ones that make you go crazy." She nodded.

"Right. These feelings are signals, and I think I know what they point to—the Circle."

"The Slayer Circle?"

Vickie then proceeded to explain how her senses were warning her of the pending danger and that she believed the family was in danger.

"Forget the family," Alexis nearly shouted. "You're the one in danger. They won't care about us. If you're right and the Circle really has targeted you, we need to figure out how to keep you safe."

The vampire shook her head. "I don't know everything yet. I don't even know if the Circle exists."

Her companion leaned back in her chair. *I forgot I never told her about this. I was protecting her from it. Maybe I should have told her a long time ago. Well, it's too late for that now, I guess.* "The Circle does exist."

"How do you know?"

"When I originally started researching all the stuff you told us after you first woke up, I found evidence online that the Circle still existed. They get together in Salzburg on a regular basis to celebrate the work of the Sang Crusade. That gut feeling you have is because they still exist."

Vickie rested her chin on her hands. "How could you have known about this and not told me?"

"I'm sorry. I didn't think it would be relevant. I honestly thought these were a weird group of losers who got together to be dorks for a month about something that happened four hundred years ago. I didn't think they would come here and try to kill you."

Both sat at the table, dumbfounded. Neither had

anything else to add until Vickie tapped the box on the table between them. "I told you my thing. What's in here?"

Her excitement was now tempered, but she was still eager to open it. "I did some research on vampires in Austria, and I came across this." She tore the box open, sifted through the bubble packs that protected the merchandise, and withdrew an ancient-looking book with yellowed pages and an ornate green cover. "I don't know any German, but I'm told this is an old journal written by an Austrian man believed to be a vampire about five hundred years ago."

She flipped the book open and saw hundreds of hand-written pages, all in German.

"Where did you get this?"

"On eBay. I don't know if it's a hoax or not, but maybe you can tell me. I wanted to surprise you with something that could connect you to the world you used to live in."

The vampire was touched. *That's a really nice gesture. I knew these were good people.* "Give it here. I should be able to tell whether or not it's genuine."

Alexis slid the book over to Vickie, who pulled it closer to her and leafed through the pages. She closed her eyes and bowed her head as she ran her fingers over the rough, ancient paper.

"It's genuine," she said. "This book came from my time, for sure. I can feel it."

"Awesome. So can you read it? I thought maybe it would give you a little more information on where you came from or vampires in general, or something."

For the next ninety seconds, Vickie flipped through the pages. Her eyes moved rapidly while she processed all the information. When she reached the end, she closed her eyes, shut the book, and took a deep breath.

"Was it a good read?" her sister asked with a smirk.

"Yes, it was. I can't believe how much information was in here. It was written by an Austrian vampire named Niklas Au."

"Does the name ring a bell?"

"No. But that's fine. Based on how he describes everything, the Sanguinarians have always been at war with vampires, even though they are so similar in genetic makeup."

"What's the war about?" Alexis was excited. *This is like a real-life mystery.*

"The human race. Apparently, the Sangs have always wanted to destroy the human race and take over the established world."

"Why?"

"Because they believe the human race is defective. Sangs and vampires have much in common, especially when it comes to super-strength. The Sangs believe that means we are a more fully evolved being. We are everything that humans are and also everything they are not. If we are better than them, why keep them around in the first place?"

Alexis ran her fingers through her hair and brushed it away from her face. "Can't we all simply coexist?"

Vickie shook her head. "Back then, anything that wandered away from the status quo was considered wrong. It wasn't our choice to be vampires or Sangs any more than it was their choice to be humans. For whatever reason, they never went along with that."

"I get that. But does that mean you have to kill us?"

She laughed. "I won't kill you. Not on purpose, anyway." She winked. "The vampires always strived for peace. We all wanted to coexist with other beings, especially the humans. We could all be one big, happy family."

"And Sangs didn't like that idea, I assume?"

"Not at all." Her tone became exasperated. "I heard a thing or two about this when I was a child, but I never paid much attention to it. The Sangs need flesh for survival—human flesh, preferably, although they eat others. So, they want to suck your blood, like Dracula. It's not only to terrify people or whatever but because that's how they survive."

"I wish everyone could know the difference between vampires and Sangs." Alexis sighed. "Why do they have to lump you all together like this? So you have to die because they're ignorant?"

"Alexis, I've been here long enough to see how people make unfair generalizations about a group of people because of the dumb actions of a few. This is nothing new. I don't know, maybe vampires could coexist with humans today. But I doubt anyone would listen to us considering how pop culture has warped the perspective of what a vampire does."

"Okay, so we have three groups—the vampires, the Sanguinarians, and the Circle. And each group wants the other one dead."

Vickie shook her head. "No, we have four groups. There are also many humans who aren't involved at all and can't be involved or we would all be dead anyway. And vampires aren't looking to kill anyone. I know I'm the only one, but I don't want anyone to die. I simply want to be left alone to live my life."

Alexis leafed through the book. "What will you do, then? Run?" She didn't want her sister-friend to leave, but if keeping her around meant she would have to die, she wanted to prepare herself for that uncomfortable reality.

"I won't run anywhere." The vampire wore a defiant look. "My senses will tell me when the Circle finds me. And when they do, I will fight back with everything I have. This isn't four hundred years ago and they can't walk around and openly murder anyone. I have a life here, and I'll protect it with all the energy and power I have inside me."

Her companion stiffened her spine. "You're not fighting this alone."

"No, no, I can't allow you to put yourself in danger." She shook her head vigorously. "That will not happen. This is my battle and this is my war. I need to be the one to fight it."

"But what if you lose? What if you confront these guys yourself and you come up short? Then what do you do? What will *I* do? They will kill you. You're family. The last thing we do in this house is let family fight alone."

Vickie admired her courage and she was flattered by her willingness to face danger to protect her. But she wouldn't forgive herself if something bad happened to Alexis. That's why she'd resolved to not tell her if and when she engaged in conflict with the Circle.

"The Circle killed the entire vampire race." Alexis had practically grabbed her by the shirt to shake her. "All the vampires and Sangs in Europe—gone. Because of these guys. You can't do this alone. That's stupid and unnecessarily dangerous. You cannot expect to overpower the same people who eliminated your entire race generations ago."

She thought about it for a moment. "You're right, but also, this is a different kind of group than the traditional Circle that existed in my day. There were likely dozens or even hundreds of Circle members before I went to sleep. Today, there can't be that many anymore. Vampires haven't posed a threat to anyone's existence, and barely anyone knows they exist nowadays too. If their numbers are down, I would be able to handle them physically."

Alexis knew she was right. Still, she wouldn't wait forever. At some point, she would have her chance to step up to the plate and protect Vickie. She merely had to keep an eye out for when this attack would take place.

And she also needed to arm herself somehow.

CHAPTER TWENTY-TWO

The classroom buzzed with excitement as students checked their cars carefully.

It was Race Day in Vickie's physical science class, and twenty students huddled around their desks to show off the vastly different models they built.

Some had carefully crafted theirs from different materials. Others were slapped together out of things they found in the garbage.

A few students focused on making their cars as small and aerodynamic as possible. Others concentrated their efforts on weight distribution so they would carry more momentum once they cruised past the bottom of the ramp.

Vickie sat at her desk, her arms folded in front of her, and studied her car. She had no help, but she felt she didn't need it. She didn't need to win anything, only do well enough to get an A.

Her car was built with a small cardboard box for a body and CDs taped together for the wheels. She made the axles out of old coat hanger wire, threaded them through the center of the CDs, and secured them with Styrofoam squares she rescued from a package delivered to Craig.

Megan Fitz scoffed as she walked past her desk. "Not the prettiest-looking car in the world, Frau."

She looked at her adversary, her expression filled with disdain. "I didn't think there were any extra credit points for looks, Megan."

The blonde held her wooden car up proudly. "If there were, there would be no point in competing. Look at this beauty. I've tweaked her wheels for a couple of weeks now. I can't wait to show you how fast she flies."

As the brattish girl walked away, Vickie rolled her eyes. Mr. Bilitz walked in and clapped with enthusiasm.

"Here we go, kids," he practically shouted. "Today is the day. I see really cool designs out there, and some I know will do really well. So, let's move this party into the hallway where we can take them all for a test drive."

Out in the corridor just outside the door, he had set up a large ramp, spray painted black. On the floor, strips of brightly colored neon masking tape marked the distance from the ramp to a measurement of a hundred and fifty feet.

"I doubt anyone will go beyond that, but if you do, rest assured, you'll earn an A. Here are the rules. You put your car at the top of the ramp, give it a little push if you want, and let gravity take it from there. But as you push, you need to keep your palm up against the ramp. This is so that you don't go overboard and game the system."

"So you can basically only push with your fingertips," one student said.

"Exactly. We'll go in alphabetical order, starting with Sarah Abel."

One by one, the students launched their cars down the ramp and across the hallway floor. One student's crashed at the bottom of the slope and almost reduced her to tears in frustration. Several traveled quite far and some even past eighty feet before they stopped.

But for every car that did well, there were two or three that puttered out at twenty feet and one veered to the right when it came off the ramp and crashed into the wall.

The students still enjoyed the activity as it was more interesting than a lecture. Mr. Bilitz enjoyed it because he loved seeing the kids apply science to a real-world project and have fun with it.

"All right, next—Megan Fitz. Let's see it, Megan."

The girl strolled casually to the ramp and gave her car a flick with her finger to send it down. Gravity pulled it at a furious pace, and the car cruised down the hallway when it reached the floor. Before it even stopped, the students cheered, impressed by how well it performed.

A few of the students ran with the car and jogged alongside it to catch the measurement. Megan flashed a cocky smile at Vickie.

"One hundred and thirty-five feet!" a student shouted when the car rolled to a stop. The class erupted in applause.

"We have ourselves a new record," Mr. Bilitz announced gleefully and noted the distance in his grade book.

Megan raised her arms in victory. "Follow *that*."

Two more students tried but they couldn't get anywhere near the new record.

Finally, it was Vickie's turn. The vampire stepped forward and placed the cardboard box car at the top of the ramp. She closed her eyes and directed a surge of super-strength through her right arm and into her hand.

With all the strength she could power behind it, Vickie shoved the car. Powered by the enhanced strength of that push, the car rocketed onto the floor.

There were no cheers. She had expected an instant wave of energy, but instead, all that could be heard was silence. Startled, she looked around and saw only wide eyes and open mouths. Of course, none were more satisfying than Megan's shocked expression.

Her car hurtled past the new record mark, past the tape, and farther down the hallway. When it finally stopped, no one knew what to do.

Mr. Bilitz stammered. "Um…okay, no one move. I'll have to get my wheel. Holy cow."

He jogged into the classroom to retrieve his measuring wheel from the closet behind his desk. While the class waited in stunned silence, he placed it at the base of the ramp, zeroed the counter, and rolled it forward to walk down the hallway until he finally reached Vickie's car.

With a smile on his face and a look of slight disbelief, he shouted to the students, "Vickie's car ran two hundred and forty-seven feet!"

That's when the cheers erupted as she had expected. She received high-fives and pats on the back from her classmates—except for Megan, of course, who glared at her while she leaned against the wall. *One step ahead. Again. It's like she wants me to be miserable.*

The teacher picked Vickie's car up and carried it back

to her while he studied it from every possible angle. "What, did you put a motor in here or something?" He laughed. "I'm only kidding. Unbelievable. You've set a record I don't think anyone will ever touch. Nice job. But looking at it, for the life of me, I can't figure out why this thing moved so far."

She thanked him and took the car into the classroom to put it on her desk. When she turned to return to the hallway to watch the others, Megan stood in the room and stared at her.

"You cheated." She put her hands on her hips.

"How?"

"I don't know. But you had to cheat. There's no way that piece of junk could have bested my car. No way."

The vampire smiled. "Your problem has nothing to do with the fact that I set a record or got an A or anything like that. The only reason you think I cheated is because I beat you."

"I have worked on my car for weeks." The girl pointed to her chest. "I have honed it, perfected it, and worked with my brother to make it the best-performing car this contest has ever seen. How do you walk in here with a cardboard box and some CDs and not only beat me, not only beat everyone, not only *set a new record*…but *double* the record? That makes no sense."

She shrugged. "I'm not a scientist. I only know how to build a car, I guess. Maybe you're not as smart as you think you are. But don't be hard on yourself. Your car went really far, too."

Megan thought steam might actually shoot out of her ears. "There's something up with you. I felt it when you threw me to the floor in the cafeteria and I feel it here too. I can't put my finger on it. But whatever it is, it's not good. I'll find out what it is."

"Well, when you do, let me know." Vickie stepped aside and walked past her. She knew what Megan was feeling, but she would never admit to it.

No one walks into a new school and immediately gets the better of everyone all the time. Good grades? Destroying everyone in class contests? Assaulting me in the cafeteria? Something is wrong with this girl. The bully was sure her suspicions were well-founded.

As Vickie walked out of the classroom, she took a deep, silent breath. Once again, someone had begun to suspect that things were not all that they seemed. She was slightly nervous about that but refused to say any more. *The more times you respond to things like that, the more trouble you'll get yourself into. It's better to keep your mouth shut and let your actions do the talking. Otherwise, you risk letting someone know that something's up.*

The rest of the class raced their cars and some of them did very well. Others crashed off the ramp. The energy level was still high because they weren't in the classroom. But after Vickie's display, most of the class assumed they wouldn't be able to compete with her, which put a slight damper on the proceedings.

At the end of the class, everyone returned to their seats and Mr. Bilitz called for a round of applause for Vickie. Everyone cheered—except for Megan Fitz, who eyed her suspiciously. *What is it about her that bothers me so much? What is wrong with her? And how can I expose it and use it against her? This is my school, not hers. She's only a visitor.*

As everyone left the classroom, Megan tossed her car in the garbage.

"What are you doing?" Vickie asked. "That's a great car."

"Yes, but it's not the best, apparently." Her voice dripped with jealousy. "There's no point in keeping it for myself. What will I do with it?"

Vickie increased her pace and walked alongside her, to the girl's very clear annoyance.

"What is it about me?" the vampire asked. "You have given me so much grief in the last few months that I'm starting to think I shouldn't even be in this school. Is that what you want?"

"I used to simply want to bust your chops a little bit, Frau," her adversary answered. "But now? Now, you're a huge pain in my butt. You've hurt me, you've shown me up, and you've embarrassed me."

"You have done all those things to me too, you know."

Megan rolled her eyes. "I don't care. I care about my car. I care about winning. I care about everyone paying attention to me."

"Everyone will pay attention to you next semester, Megan. I get to do your makeup and choose your outfit. This will be fun. I have so many ideas. You'll look so pretty."

The girl was defiant. "Whatever. You'll only be spiteful. I took you down a peg or two when you got here, and you proceeded to beat me up in the cafeteria. I have zero respect for you and anything you do, Frau. Leave me alone now."

She stopped and allowed the girl to walk ahead of her. *Does she have a point? Have I walked into this school and stolen everyone's thunder? I don't like her, but I don't need to make her feel unnecessarily bad.*

Or is she simply trying to make me feel guilty for fun? The bad news is, it's working.

Vickie wound up winning the contest, of course, and the class applauded as she collected her hundred-dollar Amazon gift card.

That night at the dinner table, Vickie asked Craig for advice on dealing with Megan Fitz.

"She sounds like a real bully." He took a sip of his milk. "You have to stand up to her. I bet she doesn't feel bad at all. She's jealous and is trying to lay a guilt trip on you to make you change your mind. Don't fall for that."

"Yes, but she will keep barking at me and trying to make my life miserable for the rest of my school year. If that's what I'm supposed to deal with in school, I'll gladly drop out and go do something else."

He sighed. "As much as my wallet would appreciate the breathing space, that won't happen. You're a great athlete, you get good grades, and you have a boyfriend. Your life is set right now. You don't need validation from other people, especially bullies like Megan Fitz. She'll never be on your side, and you have to deal with that."

Vickie didn't like that idea. But she would follow it —for now.

CHAPTER TWENTY-THREE

Alexis pulled her long, curly hair into a sloppy bun as she walked out of her bedroom. "Vickie, are you ready yet?"

The vampire emerged from her room in a pair of sweatpants and a t-shirt. "I'm ready."

"I'm not looking forward to this either." She placed her hand on Vickie's shoulder. "But this was bound to happen at some point. Just do the best you can."

"Let's go, girls," Craig stood in the kitchen with his hands on his hips.

They walked in and he rubbed his hands together with excitement. "All right, look, I know this isn't the most fun thing in the world. I don't exactly enjoy it, either. But we make the best of it. Besides, I need a little extra help with Mom not being here anymore."

He picked up a small sheet of yellow notepad paper from the counter and held it up. "This is the chores list. We'll divide this up evenly and have it done in no time. It won't take more than a couple of hours."

"Dad, Vickie's been here for months. Why start with this now?"

Craig placed the paper back on the counter. "Because I have gone easy on you girls since we got home. I've picked up all the slack around here while you focused on school. Now that we're all settled in, cleaning has to be a team sport."

Alexis rolled her eyes. She liked helping her dad and was more than willing to do things around the house. She did dishes and folded laundry often. But cleaning was not one of her favorite occupations.

"It's okay," Vickie assured them. "I need to know how to do this anyway."

"That's the spirit," he responded cheerfully and threw a rag at her. "I want you to take that rag to each room of the house and start dusting. Alexis, you too." He tossed her another.

"What will you do?" His daughter caught the rag and folded it in her hands.

"I'll follow you and vacuum. At some point, I'll show Vickie how to work that, too. We'll get rid of all this dust and have a sparkly clean house."

The girls walked into the living room, where Alexis showed her sister how to dust. "Pick stuff up, wipe under it, put stuff back. It's not a difficult job."

"If it's not so hard, why do you often complain about having to do it?"

She stopped dusting. "Because it's work. I don't have to like it, do I?" She didn't know anyone who enjoyed cleaning.

Once that room was finished, they moved to the middle

bedroom and dusted the dresser and nightstand before doing the same in both back bedrooms.

While they cleaned, the roar of the vacuum cleaner continued to grow louder as Craig cleaned the carpets.

"So, what's the latest with Will?" Vickie asked and braced herself for the answer. "Have you two been talking, or what?"

"I don't know." Alexis shrugged. "He's really private. Like, I don't have his phone number. We only talk online or FaceTime. I haven't met his family. He doesn't even talk about his family. It's really weird. I want to get to know him better but he makes it really hard to do that."

That's because he's a weird jerk and you could do a lot better. "Then why are you dating him?"

"I know you don't like him. But he can be really nice. He tells me all the time how pretty I am. And he's got really nice eyes. I'm only trying to have fun with it. Like…I don't have to put on a whole lot of pressure. We're having a good time and we leave it at that."

Nonsense. I can tell it bothers you. I wish you would be honest with me about it. You don't know if he's right for you but you want him to be right for you.

"What about Eric?" she asked. "How are things with him?"

"I love it. He's so great. He treats me well and is really fun to be around. Plus, he has friends of his own and we can all hang out. He's, like, the perfect boyfriend." *Note what I'm talking about, Alexis. Eric is everything that Will isn't. He's what a boyfriend should be.*

The other girl didn't notice the point she'd tried to make, though, so they continued dusting in silence.

Meanwhile, Craig vacuumed the carpet in the hallway and poked his head into one of the bedrooms to see the girls dusting. *It looks like Vickie's getting the hang of it. Finally, a little help around here.*

But when he looked at his daughter, he froze. *She has the sweatshirt on.*

"The sweatshirt" was an old Green Bay Packers sweatshirt that once belonged to his wife. It was a light-gray color with the Packers helmet in the middle, surrounded by *SUPER BOWL CHAMPIONS* above and below it. In the upper corner, the purple Mardi Gras-inspired Super Bowl XXXI logo was still visible, though slightly faded.

Carol had that shirt as far back as he could remember. She'd told him it was a Christmas gift in 1997, and she wore it with great pride. *I always loved how much of a Packer fan she was. And now, her daughter is wearing that shirt and looks exactly like her.*

His wife often wore that sweatshirt and a sloppy bun herself when cleaning the house. He had helped whenever he could, but she was such a stickler for details, she rarely asked him to.

He continued his task as he thought of the first time he did laundry for her. Exceedingly proud of his skills, he threw all the whites in one load of laundry and all the colors in another. At the time, her jaw dropped when she saw him walk into the living room with a basket of laundry that didn't meet her approval.

"You didn't separate these?" she gasped.

"Of course I did. I put the whites in a different load."

Carol immediately shook her head. "No, no. Towels

need to go in a different load. You should wash light towels, dark towels, clothes, and whites."

"All in different loads? Are you serious?" Craig had never done laundry like that before.

But she insisted. She bought them a laundry hamper with four different compartments. For years, they had organized their laundry that way.

He smiled when he recalled that. And despite how ridiculous he thought it was, he did it. It wasn't a hill he wanted to die on. In exchange, he never did laundry because she didn't want him to screw it up.

Ironically, now that she was gone, he still divided the laundry into four different loads. He didn't have to, but when he did it, he thought of her.

In the bedroom, Vickie picked up an alarm clock from the nightstand and dusted under it. "How often do we have to do this?"

"Basically, every week." Alexis ran the rag along the tops of some books on a shelf.

"That sounds like a lot."

"If you do it every week, it's not that big a deal. But here's a secret—I don't dust under things that don't get moved. Like these books? No one takes them off the shelf. There isn't any dust under them. So, I dust the tops, I dust the space in front of them, then I'm done."

"That doesn't sound like much of a secret."

"Yeah, well, my mom would flip if she knew I did that. I don't know how particular my dad is about cleaning, but if he's anything like her, I'd be in big trouble for cutting corners."

"Then why do you do it?" The vampire had been raised

to honor her father and mother at all times. She never questioned them or deliberately disobeyed them.

"Because taking all these books down and dusting under them would take forever. And besides, it's not like anyone notices. I don't want to live in a dump with dust everywhere. So I do what I can see. That's what matters, right?"

If you care about what you can see, why date Will? He offers nothing of value that you can see.

They dusted for a few more minutes but neither girl could shake the thought of Will from their minds.

"Vickie, I was thinking… I know Will doesn't seem to be all that great on the outside. But I really do think he's a great guy and maybe a little on the shy side. Let me work with him for a while. I think I can help him be a little more social and outgoing but I need your help."

"My help?"

"He needs to be around people. Friendly people. I have a hunch that he hides everything because he has a bad life. Maybe he's surrounded by bad influences or his family is not that good to him. If we can work together, we can be good influences on him, right?"

Alexis knew she was grasping at straws, but she didn't care. She really wanted to keep trying to date Will, and she didn't want the other girl to feel such animosity towards him.

"That's fine, Alexis, but then you need to talk to him about his hatred for me. I don't like that you're dating someone who has such anger against me for seemingly no reason. That bothers me."

"I'll talk to him, I promise. Just…please, can we go on a

double date next week? Something easy where we can all hang out? I think he'll start coming around."

From the hallway, Craig laughed and shook his head when he overheard that comment. *Nothing says, "healthy relationship" like thinking someone will "start coming around."*

On their first day of pre-marital counseling, Craig and Carol had learned all about the desire of one person to try to change the other person in a relationship.

The pastor who facilitated the counseling was adamant. "There is no chance for change. If you don't love this person right now as is, you won't ever love them because you can't guarantee that they will change. Nor will you. As the relationship moves forward, change can happen organically."

But if a couple tried to force that change, Craig knew, it would be the death knell for the relationship.

He continued to vacuum and wondered how long it would take before Will would inevitably break Alexis' heart and she would have to return her focus to the house and her family.

Craig knew it was a selfish thought and he regretted it soon after. But Will and Alexis showed no signs of a healthy relationship, and he wanted to get the heartbreak over with. The anticipation of his little girl being crushed by a boy was too much for him to bear at times.

CHAPTER TWENTY-FOUR

The entire cross country team stood in Coach Lueck's classroom and bounced on their heels while rain poured outside the window.

No one sat at the desks. Some stared out the window at the rain. Others watched the coach closely to gauge his reaction as he finished a phone call.

"Uh huh. Yeah. Okay, great. Just wanted to be sure. Yeah, I have the team right here and they're ready and waiting to get going. All right. Thanks, bye." He hung up and turned his attention to his team.

It was the day of the Conference Championship race. Lueck had looked forward to this race all season. Both Varsity teams were running well, and he felt he had a real shot at nabbing both titles that season.

The teams brimmed with confidence as well—until the rain began.

"We're not rained out, are we, Coach?" Krista asked.

He stood from his desk. "As of right now, no. The races are still on. We've all been in touch with race officials throughout the day. As long as we don't see any lightning, this meet will happen."

After a hasty cheer from the students, he proceeded to give the teams a quick rundown of racing in heavy rains, along with tips on navigating the terrain. "Some of you will fall on the downhills. Wear your longest spikes. Get as much of a grip into that ground as you can. It's your best chance to stay upright. You won't set any records today."

Micah, the boys' team captain, grumbled, "I was ready to set a personal record. This really stinks." He had trained exceptionally hard and wanted the championship race to be his peak.

"For the sake of setting PRs, I understand your disappointment, Micah. But channel that energy into the race. Listen, guys, everyone will deal with the same problems you will. Every runner out there faces the risk of falling. Everyone in your race will deal with muck and a slower terrain. It's simply the nature of the weather."

Coach was disappointed by his team's energy. Normally, their enthusiasm would be at an all-time high. But in this case, it was muddled and despondent.

"Look, I know this is frustrating, but we have one goal today—to win these races as teams. We want to walk back onto the bus holding a pair of trophies. I still believe we can do that. This is your chance to show what you're made of. To rise up when the environment is tough. We are solid runners. Let's go out there and show them that."

Eric actually looked forward to the race. He was always a fan of running in inclement weather. For some reason, the extreme nature of bad weather had a galvanizing effect. But now that his girlfriend would be watching, he envisioned himself looking tough and impressive as he crossed the finish line, drenched from head to toe in rain and mud.

The team filed out of the classroom to head to the bus. The short sprint between the door and the bus showed everyone how hard it was raining. They were drenched after being exposed to the elements for mere seconds.

"Woo!" Coach shouted as he climbed aboard, the last one on the bus. "It's invigorating out there." He wore a large, encouraging smile, although most of the team didn't return it.

Vickie didn't know how to react. She hadn't really run in the rain much and wasn't sure how it would feel when she got out onto the course. During the ride to the park, she pulled out her racing shoes and changed the spikes on the bottom to the longest ones she had.

Eric sat beside her and tapped his foot with anxious energy.

"Are you okay?" she asked him.

"Oh, yeah. But I know Coach is looking for a big win today. This is our chance to take the Conference Championship. I've always wanted to be a part of a winning team."

"You've never won anything before?"

He shook his head. "No. I came from a really small grade school. We were bad at sports, so we never won anything there. This is my first real opportunity."

She grabbed his hand. "You'll do great. You'll be wet, of course, but you'll be great."

He smiled at her. "You will do great, too. It'll be fun out there."

Vickie watched the rain pummel the bus window as it lumbered along the road. *I hope it's fun. If I discover I don't like being wet all the time, this will definitely be a miserable experience.*

The vehicle pulled up to a stop at the curb. Coach Lueck stood to address the team one more time before they exited and faced the challenge ahead.

"I have our canopy set up outside the bus here. There are picnic tables under it. Make sure you place all your belongings onto those tables. Everything else is mud. Then, we'll have to go out for our warmups and run-throughs. Keep your gear on and zipped tight, and let's get out there."

One by one, the team disembarked and sprinted through the downpour until they were under the relative safety of the canopy.

Once everyone was there, the girls pulled their already wet hair into ponytails. Some of the boys squinted as the water splashed on them from outside the canopy. The whole team huddled together.

"All right, Clear Lake." Coach clapped vigorously. "Let's do our run-through. Girls, we'll go first. Micah, give the guys about ten minutes and then do yours. Races start soon, so we gotta get moving."

Each girl took a deep breath before they stepped out into the rain. They jogged lightly through the course. On the steep downhill, several slid unexpectedly. Although they managed to stay on their feet, they still felt uneasy about the ground.

Once they reached the finish line, they jogged to the canopy where Coach could address them one more time before the race. "I'll be out announcing splits. Girls, we have a real chance to win this one. I want you to go out there and give it everything you have. Lay it all out on the course and leave it there. Let's bring a trophy home."

Despite the cold, damp air under the canopy, the girls had to ditch their gear and prepare to go to the starting line. A few had wisely worn tights under their shorts, although Vickie's legs were bare.

"Aren't you gonna be cold?" Shannon asked her.

"I don't really have a choice now. Besides, once I get going, I'll be fine."

They lined up at the starting line and the gun went off. The girls ran hard out of the gate and tried to set a competitive pace from the beginning. Vickie hung back as she usually did in her focused effort to fit in while she also tried to keep herself warm. Not even a tenth of a mile into the race, she was soaked to the bone and her shoes squished with every step.

Despite this, she pushed on, raced down the line, and picked runners off as she progressed. Before she knew it, she was behind the fourth member of her own team, so she backed off slightly and ran behind her to avoid discouraging her.

The runners largely left each other alone, in stark contrast to the previous meet where Vickie had been spiked. Everyone was already exhausted from running in the mud, and the rain provided enough of a distraction to keep everyone focused on the race and the unstable course rather than the competition.

When she reached the downhill stretch, Vickie had completely forgotten about being careful. Her feet slipped out from under her and she tumbled backward into the mud.

She slid down the hill on her butt, and as she reached the bottom, her head flipped forward and she tumbled into a somersault for good measure.

With a groan, the vampire pushed herself to her feet. *How did that happen? Come on, keep going, girl. Make Coach proud.*

She ran a little faster and tried to use a bare vestige of her powers without being too obvious. It worked. By the end of the race, she had caught up to the fourth girl again, and the two of them ran side by side until they reached the finish line to a wave of cheers from those who braved the rain to watch.

Coach Lueck waited for them on the other side of the tunnel, where their tickets were torn off their numbers. He patted them both on the back. "That was real racing out there, girls. Nice work. I think we have a good chance to win this trophy."

The boys' race went well also, although no one would know the final scores and standings until the awards presentation. Vickie was very proud of how hard Eric ran. He even managed to set a personal record despite the weather—the only member on either team to accomplish that particular feat on such a rainy day.

When he finished the race, he looked like he always imagined it. He was covered in mud with even a dollop of it smeared across his forehead. Most of the blue of his uniform was brown, and the front of his shirt was caked so badly with it, she couldn't see what school he was from.

He was tired but he made good time and was happy with the effort he'd put in. He and Vickie walked into the park's pavilion, where the runners could remain under shelter while the awards were announced.

"Do you think we won it?" she asked.

"I have a good feeling about it, yeah." He nodded. "There's only one way to find out, though. I'm really rooting for Coach too. I know how badly he wants to see us achieve this."

Coach Lueck sat nervously with his clipboard. "It'll be close…" he muttered as he tallied the scores he could.

Minutes later, the girls' cross country team from Clear Lake High School was announced as the Conference Champions for that year. The runners cheered and even Vickie—who didn't understand the significance of being a champion—was excited, mainly because all the other girls were.

They each received a medal, and the team was also awarded a trophy they would present to the school during assembly.

The boys' team was much closer in points, but by a margin of three, Clear Lake won the boys' race too.

Coach Lueck was overjoyed. He took picture after picture during the entire evening to enthusiastically document the day when he finally reached the goal he'd carried close to his heart for years—double Conference Champions.

Vickie knew she had played a huge part in it, and she was proud of that too, even if no one else noticed or even mentioned it.

As she sat on the bus to go home, she glanced at the medal hanging around her neck. *You're a winner. You joined a team and you won it all. This is a big day for you.*

"Hey, nice medal." Eric smiled at her as he approached her seat. "Do you mind if I hop in here?"

"Not at all," Vickie said. "Any seat is open for a fellow champion." They clinked their medals together playfully as the bus barreled down the road to the high school with champions aboard.

CHAPTER TWENTY-FIVE

Craig was taking notes in his bedroom, scribbling ideas for *The Truth About... The Real Modern Family* and how he could make it work, when the girls walked in.

"Dad, can we have a second?"

He spun in his chair. "Of course, girls, what's up?"

"Um, Friday night, Will and Eric want to take us out on a double date." Alexis folded her hands in front of her. "Do you think we could go?"

His heart sank. *I knew this day was coming but I don't know if I'm ready for it yet. Still, telling them not to go because I'm not ready would be really selfish. They're old enough.*

"Where will you go?"

"Bruegger's."

Bruegger's Bagels was a small bagel shop around the corner from the high school. It was another popular hangout for the kids, especially in the mornings before school. Aside from the brisk breakfast trade, it was open normal restaurant hours and served bagel sandwiches for lunch and dinner.

It's a public place and a familiar place so it's not the worst plan in the world. Plus, they're doubling up, so there's less of a chance of anything happening that I wouldn't approve of.

"I think that would be okay. Do you need a ride?"

"Actually, Eric's mom will take us. You're off the hook."

Her father smiled. At least he didn't have to listen to the high school kids' chatter like he had at Homecoming. "Be home by ten."

The girls smiled and high-fived before they strolled out of the room. Craig spun back to his desk and glanced out the window to the back yard, which he could see from his desk.

My little girl's first real date. Wow.

It was a milestone moment for both the girls and their father. He thought back to some of his first dates.

How many movies and restaurants have I been to on dates? Especially first dates? Oh, and crazy Rebekah Weigand.

She was the sister of a friend of his. Years before, he met her and thought she was cute. He had invited her to his apartment to watch a movie one night and came to regret it minutes later.

They tried to watch the movie, but she talked through most of it. His roommate was building a scale model for his architecture class and was cutting foam with a scalpel. She asked if she could play with it. Thankfully, he refused.

After she'd annoyed them both thoroughly for a few hours, she went home. Craig decided to take her out on one more date—dinner, this time, where he could let her down easy.

Instead, he picked her up and she decided she wanted

to go to a movie—and told him she knew he intended to break up with her.

Ugh. We only went out on one date. And then I was starving but had to pay to see a movie with a girl who I didn't want to be around and who hated me. Those were seriously the most awkward few hours of my life.

It was because of that experience that he instituted a new rule entitled, "Gauge The Crazy Drinks." When he thought he had a chance with Carol, he didn't want to rush into anything. Instead, he asked her out for a drink—less of a commitment, easy to break off if things went south, and enough opportunity to talk and get to know one another.

To his delight, she passed with flying colors.

She drank water the whole night. I loved that about her. As a guy who was broke, knowing I didn't need to pay for too many drinks was a huge step in the right direction. Man, she was great.

The two talked for hours. Craig had a few drinks, but she stuck with water all night long. At the end of it, they parted ways, and the next day, he called her to set up a real date.

He chuckled when he thought about it.

I had her come over to my place so I could make her dinner. I couldn't afford to take her out anywhere. The plan was that we could watch a movie at my house, eat dinner there, and enjoy each other's company without having to spend an arm and a leg. And she was up for it.

It went as well as any first date could go. One year later, they were engaged. The year after that, they were married.

For a moment, Craig worried if the same thing would happen to his daughter. *If she did that, she'd be married by the time she got out of high school.* He shook his head. *That's ridiculous. That won't happen. Besides, it wouldn't even be legal to get married that young. Your mind is playing tricks on you, boy.*

Four years after he and Carol got married, she gave birth to Alexis. She was a perfect baby and made her arrival in the world a few minutes after seven a.m. on a Thursday morning. *The longest night of my life. Everything changed when I held that girl for the first time.*

But when he thought about that day, he thought of the few minutes before she came out.

He sat at his wife's side and held her hand. The nurses had called the doctor in, and they were ready for her to push. One nurse dimmed the lights, leaned over, and whispered, "Enjoy these last few moments of only the two of you together."

Craig smiled and choked up when he thought of that moment in the dim morning light, holding his wife's hand as they prepared to become a family. At the time, they were both silent with lumps in their throats and stomachs twisted with nervousness.

They hadn't realized how different the world would be, and how that was the end of it all.

Of course, from there, they experienced a new beginning and a new life together with their daughter. It was a life they loved—one they cherished every single day.

And now, that little baby girl was going to go off on her first date, starting down the journey of finding someone to hold her hand before she gave birth someday. *That's a long way away, man. Don't let yourself get caught up in that.*

It was as if, in that moment, he had to deal with that new beginning experience all over again. Once his daughter started dating, nothing would be the same.

It never failed. Any time he thought of that moment in the hospital, the last few minutes of life as they had known it, he thought of holding his wife's hand in hospice care.

While she took laboring breaths and her frail body finally gave out on her, he held her hand again like he had done before. But the circumstances were so very different.

When Alexis was born, those moments were filled with anticipation—an appreciation for the time they had and looking forward to the new life they would have. But in hospice, the moments overflowed with grief.

There wouldn't be any new life together. He held her hand as she prepared to leave. It was a new life by subtraction, not by addition.

In either case, nothing would be the same. At some point on both occasions, he had to let go of her hand. Life had to move on. He couldn't sit in the past anymore, whether he wanted to or not.

Craig pushed away from his desk and walked to the kitchen for a glass of water. While he was there, Alexis walked through on her way to the basement. After taking a sip, he walked over to her.

"What's up, Dad?"

Without saying a word, he grabbed her arm and lifted her hand in his. She stared at him like he was a crazy person while he held her hand to his chest and stared at her.

"Dad, are you okay?"

He squeezed her hand once, took a deep breath, and let it go. Still unsure of what that was all about, Alexis continued slowly to the basement.

He sighed and put his hands in his pockets. Then, he walked to the patio door and looked out at the field. *From this moment on, it all changes again. A new stage in life. You've survived these before and you can do it again.*

"Are you all right?"

Craig turned his head to see Vickie standing behind him. "Oh, I'm fine, Vickie. Thanks. Just thinking."

"About what?" She knew something was bothering him and that he was dealing with a touch of the grief in his soul.

"Changes."

"Like?"

"Just…life changes. Alexis is going on her first real date. It's a big deal for me."

"Why?" She stepped up beside him and stared out the window too.

"Well…because it's a big change for everyone. She'll go out on more dates after this. It'll be a much bigger part of her life. It's hard to understand, but I'll have a hard time setting my little girl free so she can go off to date boys."

Vickie smiled at how much he cared for his daughter. She remembered the warmth that came from her own father. "Alexis will always be your little girl. She only wants to grow up. We all do. Time marches on."

"I guess I can't talk to you about how life changes. You underwent more than your fair share."

"Of course I did." She nodded. "But I survived. So will

you. Besides, Alexis doesn't want to lose you. She's already having a hard enough time without her mom. She'll go on some dates because that's what kids our age do, but she'll always come home and be your daughter."

CHAPTER TWENTY-SIX

Alexis stood in front of the bathroom mirror to apply, re-apply, and tweak her makeup. *This is stupid. We're only going to Bruegger's. I don't know why I'm obsessing so much.*

She took a step back and stared at her outfit. She had worn her favorite burgundy long-sleeved shirt over a white cami and her good pair of jeans. *Is this too dressy? Not dressy enough? Should I look fancier for my first date? No, that would make you look like you're trying too hard.*

"Is everything okay?" Her father stopped in the doorway with a sympathetic smile on his face.

"Oh, hey, Dad. Yeah, I'm fine. Just…"

"Nervous?"

"Yeah. And I don't know why. I've been to Bruegger's a hundred times. Now, because Will's going to be there, I have to be all nervous about it? Is this normal?"

He laughed. "It's way more normal than you think. You know, when I went on my first date back in high school, I was paranoid about my hair."

"Your hair? Why? You're a boy."

"Well, yeah, but hair was a big deal for the guys back then too." He folded his arms and leaned casually against the doorway. "At the time, I was a gel man. I wore hair gel every day. The biggest trend was to spike only the front of your hair with everything else pulled forward. It sounds simple enough but the problem was, I couldn't get it to look right. I kept adding gel to try to make it sit perfectly, and it wouldn't. So, I'd duck my head under the bathroom faucet, rinse the gel out, and start over again. Honestly, I think it took me, like, forty-five minutes to do my hair for my first date."

Alexis laughed and the tension in her body released. "That's terrible. I didn't think boys spent that much time in front of the mirror."

"I did, yeah. And even better, all that washing and re-gelling and re-styling made me really sweaty. I was a sweaty kid, to begin with. After I got my hair all perfect, I had to change my shirt because my pits were soaked. Of course, that messed my hair up, and I had to style it all over again."

"Dad, this is an awful story. Did your date notice?"

He shrugged. "She never commented on any of it. I didn't know at the time, but that's because she already wanted to go out on the date. While I was getting ready, I was looking for reasons why she might not want to be with me. She didn't do that. Do you get my point?"

She looked into the mirror. "How do I stop being so nervous about this stuff?"

Craig stepped forward, put his arm around her shoulders, and squeezed her tightly. "You don't."

"Well, that's reassuring."

"Hey, I'm merely being honest. But even though I know you won't listen to me, I'll say it. You look beautiful, and Will agreed to this date because he wants to be there. Don't overthink it. Go out and have fun."

"Thanks, Dad."

He walked out of the room, whistling, and she touched her makeup up one more time.

When she was done, she walked out to the living room to see Vickie sitting on the couch, totally relaxed.

"You're not nervous?"

"Why should I be nervous?" She felt comfortable with Eric and she wasn't too worried about her appearance.

Soon, their ride pulled up in the driveway. The girls said goodbye to Craig and walked out the door, where the boys waited in the back of her van. He stood at the front door and waved at Eric's mom.

They drove off and he stared at the car until it disappeared down the road. *That's it. Nothing will ever be the same ever again.*

The drive to Bruegger's was very similar to the drive to Homecoming. The girls talked non-stop and Eric jumped in whenever he could. Will stayed mainly quiet and simply watched everyone else talk.

This irritated Vickie almost beyond endurance. *We're doing this again? Seriously? Why bother with this date?*

They reached their destination and the two couples scrambled out of the van. "Text me when you want me to pick you up, Eric. Have fun, guys."

Bruegger's was not very busy that night but the aroma

of freshly toasted bagels hung in the air and everyone was hungry.

"I haven't been here at night," Alexis said. "I usually get a bacon-egg-cheese bagel if I come here, but that's breakfast. What do you have for dinner?"

"The chicken salad is really good," Eric told them. "I bet the ham is, too."

"What will you have, Will?" Vickie hated talking to him and he seemed as disgusted by it as she was. But she wanted Alexis to have a good time, especially if he wouldn't make any effort.

"Nothing."

"Aren't you hungry?" Alexis asked him. He shook his head. "Okay…will you simply sit and watch us eat?"

"It's fine. I wanted to come. I don't need to eat."

After ordering their bagels, they each filled their cups with soda and waited at a table until their number was called. Once it was ready, Eric and Alexis both walked over to pick it up.

Seated across from Will, Vickie leaned over. "Hey," she whispered. "Can you please be a part of this date?"

"You don't want me to."

"No, I don't. But Alexis does. I'm doing this for her. Why don't you suck it up and involve yourself in the conversation?"

He sneered at her, then switched to a fake smile when Alexis arrived. This gave the girl a small confidence boost as it was the first time he'd smiled at her while they were out.

"How does everyone feel about their grades this

semester?" she asked before she bit into a chicken salad bagel.

"I know I got an A in physical science." Vickie smiled and picked up her ham and cheese bagel.

"Most of my classes were pretty good," Eric answered.

Alexis turned and looked at Will. "What about you, Will? How are your grades? As the new kid in school, I wondered how you had adapted."

He tried not to look at the vampire. "I think my grades will be fine."

Alexis nodded, a little disappointed because she'd expected more to the response than he'd volunteered. "Well, that's good," she said and sounded a little despondent.

They all ate in silence for a few minutes.

"What should we do after this?" Vickie asked.

"I thought we could walk over to La Follette Park," Eric answered.

"Ugh! La Follette." Vickie scoffed.

He laughed. "Don't worry, we're not doing that."

La Follette Park was located about a mile away from the high school. The loop around the entire park was roughly half a mile, which made it the perfect place for the cross country team to conduct workouts. The problem was that the middle of it had a long, winding, steep hill that soared almost vertically.

It was another park with a reputation for breaking runners with tough, puke-inducing workouts.

She wasn't bothered by the park. However, almost everyone else on the team hated it. To fit in, she had to pretend as though the La Follette workouts were torture.

"There's a playground on one side with tennis courts," Eric said. "Plus, there's the big open space in the middle. Maybe there will be a game going on or something." He shrugged easily. "I thought it was something to do that's close by, and we don't have any licenses."

The group wolfed down the rest of their bagels and walked out the front door to head to their next destination. First, they had to walk past the front of the high school.

"I know we spend a lot of time here, but it always looks and feels so different at night," Eric observed. "Like…it's a different building."

Vickie nodded. "The atmosphere changes after hours."

They walked a few paces ahead of Alexis and Will, who trailed them in silence. She could feel Will's anger burning, and he stared into her back with enough heat that she could sense it. She turned to scowl at him, but he merely continued his expressionless stare.

He will ruin this date, ruin Alexis' good time, and be an awful person. Man, I wish she could have enough confidence to dump him.

They turned the corner and headed up to the park. Vickie and Eric laughed as he told stories of being pelted with crabapples picked off the trees that lined the street— another initiation for freshmen on the cross country team.

The vampire glanced over her shoulder to where Alexis looked uncomfortable and awkward. She obviously wanted to have more fun but was unable to because of her date. *I want to help her, but I don't. She needs to see this guy is wrong for her, and I can't distract from that. She has to see it for herself.*

They reached La Follette Park and to their delight, an intramural game of Ultimate Frisbee was taking place in the middle of the park.

Vickie, of course, had no idea what game they were playing. Eric dutifully explained the rules to her as they watched two teams sling the hot pink disc to each other as they sprinted up and down the field.

They cheered when teams scored, and the players seemed to appreciate having an audience to watch them for a change.

"That looks like a lot of fun," she said. "Maybe we should play that sometime."

"I'm surprised you haven't already. It's one of Coach Lueck's favorite games." Eric then told them about the time he took a frisbee to the side of his head during one of those games, which were normally played during summer practices.

The group moved on to the playground where they swung on the swings like little kids. Will sat on one without really swinging on it. For some weird reason, he seemed to staunchly refuse to have any fun. Instead, he stared at Vickie.

Alexis looked close to tears as she dealt quietly with a date who seemed completely disinterested in her.

The vampire fumed in silence, although she tried to keep a smile on her face. *I can't take this much longer. He has to go. What is his problem? And why is he so fixated on me?*

It wasn't a romantic thing. That much she knew for sure. Will was a man of his word and he truly hated her. She could sense that but simply had no idea why.

And in the meantime, her friend was tortured by it because she assumed Will wanted nothing to do with her.

As far as Vickie could tell, she was right. But that still didn't explain why he insisted on dating her.

CHAPTER TWENTY-SEVEN

That evening, after the date, Alexis was fairly quiet. Eric's mom dropped them off at the house and she walked past the living room and into her room to close the door behind her.

Craig looked at Vickie, who walked into the living room. "How was the date? Is Alexis okay?"

She shrugged as she slumped onto the couch. "I don't know. The date was fine. Eric and I had fun. But Will is… well, he's weird. I don't really know how else to describe it. He doesn't really seem to like Alexis. I don't know why he keeps going on dates with her."

"She's probably struggling with a little heartache, then." He winced and felt bad for his little girl for having to deal with that so soon. "That's a pain I'm familiar with."

"I want to help her." She put one leg up on the couch. "She should be allowed to have a good time too, right?"

"I'm her father, so I obviously think she should. But you can't really help her on this one. All you can do is let her figure it out."

"You know what I'm talking about with Will, though. You've met him."

"He gives me a weird vibe." He nodded. "But at the same time, if I start trying to influence her decisions like that, it won't go well."

"Why not? Shouldn't she honor her father?"

Man, if all daughters could be like you. "Sure, she should. But she's also growing up and that means she wants to be more independent. It's natural. If I try to break her and Will up, she will dig in her heels more. That will only make things worse because her relationship will be out of spite and it'll take forever for them to realize it won't work. It's far better to hang back and give her time and space to learn for herself."

"I don't understand that. If you're the father and you know better, you should be able to tell her."

Craig didn't bother to reply because he knew she wouldn't understand. "But things are going well with you and Eric, hey?"

"He's really sweet." She smiled. "And a lot of fun. I feel comfortable around him."

"Don't get too comfortable. He is still a teenage boy."

Alexis didn't come out of her room for the rest of the evening. Her father poked his head into her room to say goodnight and make sure she was okay. To his surprise, she wasn't crying, but she didn't look happy either.

In the middle of the night, he woke up to go to the bathroom. As he walked out of his room, he decided to get a drink of water, too. He stumbled down the hallway, a little clumsy because he tried to keep his eyes closed so he wouldn't wake up too much.

He filled a glass and stood at the sink while he drank quickly. After the last gulp, he sighed and placed it on the counter.

That was when he heard a cracking noise coming from outside. Confused, he opened his eyes fully and walked over to the patio window, from where he saw two young men breaking into the side door of the garage with a crowbar.

They managed to force the door open and ran in. Without thinking his next steps through fully, Craig ran to the counter above the sink and smacked the automatic garage door opener in the hope that it would scare them away.

The large door opened, and the two young men froze in the middle of the garage. They were dragging his snow-blower out from the shed.

The two of them raced out of the garage and saw him through the patio window. Again, he froze.

One of them drew a gun and fired it at him. The glass shattered, and he dropped to the floor and crawled over to the kitchen table. Another gunshot fired through the wreckage and embedded itself in the wall of the kitchen.

Alexis and Vickie both ran out of their rooms. Vickie saw what was happening and instantly, her senses kicked in. "Get back in your room," she ordered Alexis. "Dad, stay down."

She sprinted to the patio door and hurdled through the broken aperture to land on the patio in front of the invaders. Without even a second's hesitation, the gunman fired and a bullet plowed into her shoulder.

"Vickie!" Craig yelled.

The force of the shot knocked her back, but she stayed calmly on her feet and stared at the gunman. He became paralyzed with fear when he saw that the bullet did nothing to her.

Instead, she flexed her shoulder and slowly, the bullet was pushed out of her skin. It fell to the concrete with a clinking noise.

"Shoot her again!" his accomplice shouted.

He obliged and this time, aimed at her head. Vickie reached up and caught the bullet with her bare hand before she dropped it casually. She smiled at them, and they trembled in response.

Now, it was her turn.

She launched her first charge at the gunman, shoulder first, and pounded into him with such force that he catapulted into the wooden fence on the other side of the driveway about fifteen feet away. He sprawled on the pavement and clutched his broken ribs.

As his accomplice stared at his friend, his knees practically knocking together, Vickie reached over with one hand, grasped his arm, and snapped it. He squealed and fell into a seated position, and tears filled his eyes.

"You picked the wrong house to rob." She drove her knee into his face. The sharp blow broke his nose and knocked him unconscious.

Vickie walked casually back to the house. Under the table, Craig shook his head in disbelief.

"I…uh… Wow…thank you?"

She smiled at him. "Are you okay?"

"Yeah. Yeah, they didn't get me."

"Cool. Call the cops. I'll check on Alexis."

Without taking his eyes off the two burglars in his driveway, Craig dialed nine-one-one. Minutes later, two squad cars arrived and saw the carnage.

"You made this job easy for us," one officer said. "So, what happened?"

Craig explained to them that the two young men had broken into his garage and were in the process of stealing some of his things.

"And you attacked them?"

"They shot at me after seeing me, and—"

Vickie walked up behind him. "They missed their first shot, and he ran out there and fought them both. I think they were so scared, they couldn't aim properly. They didn't have a chance. I watched the whole thing from under the table. He was brilliant."

The officer nodded while he took notes. "Sir, I appreciate the fact that you were defending your family. But I also want to remind you that this is not normally the way to solve these issues. You could have been seriously hurt. Thank goodness you got the better of them, or these girls would have lost their father tonight."

"Um…yes officer. I understand."

"Now, that said, well done. In this particular situation, it definitely worked out for you. We'll tell everyone down at the precinct about these guys."

They called for medical assistance, and an ambulance arrived shortly thereafter. The EMTs hunched over them and made a preliminary examination of the prisoners.

"Good grief," one of them exclaimed. "Did you run him over with your car? I haven't seen so much damage from a one-on-one fight before. His ribs are shattered."

The other one concurred. "This kid's arm feels like it was bashed in by a baseball bat. Unbelievable."

They loaded them into the ambulance. After speaking with the EMTs, one of the officers returned to Craig. "Did you use some kind of weapon, sir?"

"Ah, no…only my fists." *That sounded really corny. You panicked, doofus. Way to sound like a dork.*

The officer laughed. "You should have those things registered as weapons. You definitely did a number on them. I haven't seen as much damage as this before."

After they cleaned up and left, Craig and the girls sat in the living room and tried to come down from the two a.m. adrenaline rush.

"Thank you, Vickie, but why didn't you tell the officers that it was you?"

"Are you kidding?" She thought the question was ridiculous. "If a grown man does that much damage, it's interesting and impressive. If a fourteen-year-old girl does that much damage, it becomes a news story. People talk about me. I get more unwanted attention. It's the exact opposite of what I want, isn't it?"

"I don't know why I didn't think of that," Craig said. A cold rush of air flew through the broken window. "We'll need to have that replaced. It sure seems like ever since we brought a vampire into the house, I have to constantly do home repairs." He chuckled.

"Hey, you can't blame that one on me." Vickie laughed. "I would've opened the door and run out there instead."

"Lex, are you okay?"

"Yeah, I'm all right. I wish I could have seen it happen, though."

"I'm glad you didn't. Not because it wasn't fun to watch. It really was. But when there's a gunman out in my drive-way, I want my daughter as far away as possible." He stood and walked over to her to sweep her into a hug.

She responded warmly. "I'm glad they were terrible shots, then. I'm really not interested in losing another parent this year."

The vampire smiled. "I'll do what I can to make sure you don't have to worry about that."

CHAPTER TWENTY-EIGHT

Craig dragged the desk in his bedroom away from the wall and into the middle of the room. *This will feel weird. I never do podcasts in person.*

Vickie walked in and pushed the desk chair from her room to the other side of the table while he plugged in the second microphone. She sat and rocked casually as she waited for them to get started.

He sat, scanned the notebook page where he had jotted down a few notes, nodded to himself, then plopped it on the table in front of her. "Okay, here are some notes to remind you of some of the things we talked about. If you freeze up, you can simply check the notes."

"Okay." She looked a little hesitant. "Will everyone hear us right away? How does this work? Do I have to sit a certain way?"

Craig laughed. "Lean forward so your mouth is about this close to the microphone." He positioned his mouth about an inch away from his. "That way, it'll pick you up clearly. And no, it's not live or anything. We'll record this."

She pointed to his laptop. "Our voices will go into there?"

"Yep. And after it's recorded, I can edit anything out. Don't worry about saying the wrong thing. I can clean it up in post, as they say. Relax and have fun. The best podcasts in the world are very conversational. That's the tone I'm going for here."

She took a loud, deep breath. "Why am I so nervous?"

"Because it's new and it's something you don't understand. Remember, it's okay to make mistakes. We'll edit them out later. Be yourself and enjoy it. Ready?"

He clicked the big red *RECORD* button on his laptop and began to speak. "Hey, everyone, and welcome to Season three of *The Truth About...* with Craig Watson. I *am* Craig Watson, and I'm thrilled to be back here for another season with all of you. If you're new to the show, I am a former investigative journalist. On this show, I choose a topic and go deeper than the headlines in an attempt to uncover the real truth the media may be hiding from you. Today, we start a new season titled, *The Truth About... The Real Modern Family*. I know this is a departure from the first two seasons, but I thought it would be a lot of fun to dig into a topic that...well, a lot of you can relate to. I'm also excited because this season, we will have a regular guest contributor, a lovely young woman named Vickie. How are you doing today, Vickie?"

Unsure of what to do next, she pointed to her microphone. Craig nodded and waved for her to lean forward. "I...I'm doing fine, thank you."

He gave her a thumbs-up. "The reason she will join us as our special guest throughout Season three is because she is a brand-new member of my family. We've gone through significant changes around here—including the loss of my wife, which is a topic for another day—and during the healing process, we brought someone new into the house. What's your background, Vickie?" He pointed to the notebook.

Vickie slid the notebook closer so she could read it into the microphone. "Well, I am formerly from Salzburg, Austria, and I am a distant cousin to you and your daughter. I wanted to move to the United States, and am now a citizen here and living with the two of you."

"That's right. Vickie is an adopted daughter of mine, and we are thrilled to have her here with us. Now, to confirm for everyone listening, although you are from Austria, you are not currently wearing a dirndl, correct?"

She laughed. "No, that's not something I do. In fact, that's not something most Austrian girls do at all. But I'm sure we'll talk about that."

"We absolutely will." *She's doing great so far. Every time she speaks, she gets a little more comfortable. Keep it up.* "Now, what made you want to come to America in the first place?"

Vickie looked at her notebook again. "I don't want to get too political on this podcast, because I don't think that's helpful to anyone, but I was looking for a change. There were certain things happening in my homeland that made me feel…under pressure, let's say. I wanted freedom from that, so America seemed to be the perfect choice."

"That is great. And we've worked to help you feel like this is home. What do you think is the biggest struggle of being here so far?"

She nodded, slid the notes back to him, and started to understand what kinds of answers he was looking for. "Not being with my parents. They were taken from me at a young age, so I had the freedom to do this. But even though we're navigating the 'new normal,' I do still think of them often and… well, I miss them."

She's a pro already. "You're living with my daughter, Alexis, now, who's the same age as you. Do you have any big differences that you two struggle to deal with? We'll have her on soon as well, but I'm curious as to your point of view."

"Let's see…do I have to only pick one?" They both laughed. "Being from Austria, I have quickly grown very tired of The Sound of Music. We have tours there, and people from all over the world come to see the places where they filmed that movie." Vickie looked at Alexis. *In the short time I've been awake.* Alexis knew what she was thinking and gave her an encouraging smile. "Alexis is a big fan of that movie and its music, so I occasionally have to suffer through listening to Edelweiss again, even though I couldn't get away from it at home, either."

"You know, it's kinda funny. We've known each other for a little while now"—*to say the least*—"and it never occurred to me that one of Alexis' favorite movies would be your least favorite. We even did the Sound of Music tour when we visited Austria. I've never seen the movie, though."

Vickie giggled. "Yes, and I try to be okay with that. It's not her fault that I'm tired of it. She's allowed to have her favorites even if I disagree with them."

Craig raised a finger. "Now, we'll go into a lot of those

differences in future episodes because…well, we have different backgrounds. Alexis and I have spent her whole life together, and we come from the same point of view on many things. That's something that you tend to take for granted in a blended family."

"Absolutely. It's tempting to think that everyone approaches life in the same way you are. But that's not the case. And I'm sure things have changed for you both since losing your wife. There are many hurdles we have to jump over as a family together."

He nodded. "And we'll get into that in more detail later in the series, for sure."

For the next hour, they discussed various challenges an international member of the family faced when coming to a new country and a new family at the same time.

After they finished recording, Craig gave her a high five. "That was awesome. You did great. You seemed a little nervous at the start, but you got into the rhythm and never looked back. Good for you."

"It was fun." Vickie was beaming. *Another unique new experience for me.* "So what happens now?"

"I'll edit it a little to clip out a few lines and some silences so it flows better. Then, I'll release it in a few days. I've set aside a little money to advertise the episode on social media. I think the whole blended family angle will attract new listeners."

"And new listeners means more money, right?"

"Right. More listeners means I can charge more for an ad spot. It's a big deal. This topic is so far from what I'm used to talking about, and I honestly think it'll work.

Running ads will give it a little extra juice to push it to the top."

That night, Craig finished the episode and scheduled ads to run on the major social media platforms.

Two days after the release of the episode, he logged into his podcasting account to take a look at the numbers. He was nervous but excited to see how well everything did. His ads had performed very well, and a significant number of eyeballs saw the podcast.

But did they listen to the episode?

Once he saw the report, he stood and immediately knocked on Vickie's bedroom door.

"Come in." He opened it quickly. "Oh, hey. What's up?"

"Vickie, I took a look at the ad numbers for our new episode."

She sat up hastily, her expression both excited and a little panicked. "You have my attention. How did we do?"

His voice gradually grew louder until he yelled, "We had...*fifty thousand listeners!*" He pumped his fist and literally jumped up and down like a kid.

The vampire was excited too although she didn't really know why. "Is that good?" she asked when he paused for breath.

"Let's put it this way. At fifty thousand listeners per episode, we can run ads that pay us one thousand five hundred dollars apiece. If I run two ad slots, we make three thousand dollars per episode. And if we run one episode a week..."

Vickie did the math in her head. "Whoa!"

"You're darn right, whoa! We have ourselves a success

on our hands. Vickie, this is great. We're in. You've saved my career."

They high-fived excitedly. "I can't believe that many people want to hear about my Austrian heritage."

"People like to hear about stuff that's out of the ordinary, and that's you. It's great, isn't it? All you have to do is show up and be yourself with a few small tweaks. Family life can be such a great niche and I knew we'd find an audience. I didn't think it would be this quickly, though."

She shook her head in disbelief. "What do we do now?"

"We keep recording—do what we're doing, try to stay as interesting as possible, and I'll keep running those ads with each episode. As long as we can keep this number that high, we'll be rolling."

Vickie cocked an eyebrow. "And I'll get a cut of this money, right?"

Craig smiled and nodded. "Of course. You're a big part of the success so it's only fair. Look at you. Now, you have your first American twenty-first century job on top of everything else."

After one more high five, he stepped out of the bedroom and walked to the kitchen where he stood for a long moment and looked out the window. *Fifty thousand listeners. I can't believe we got this going. I hope we can keep it up.*

CHAPTER TWENTY-NINE

Vickie was flying high on her new life as a podcast guest. She knew they weren't making money yet, but with their audience, Craig was confident that he could woo new advertisers fairly quickly.

And with that much money coming in, she would be able to collect a nice little income.

The fact that she could even make any money simply by talking into a microphone was mind-boggling to her. *I don't have to learn a trade or work the fields? I don't even understand why people will pay us so much money, but I definitely won't argue with it.*

Even more delightful for her was the fun she could now have on the online forums. She wanted to know what people were interested in, so she found a blended-family-focused forum and joined it. Every other post on the board was about the new podcast. Clearly, Craig had done an excellent job of delivering ads to this niche audience.

The posts were almost universally complimentary toward them, and the overall feeling among the listeners was that this would open new perspectives on blended families, and the "modern family" dynamic.

In a move she would later regret, she jumped onto the forum and began to reply to posts under her VickieVampire screen name and admitted to everyone on the board that she was, in fact, the Vickie on the podcast.

Minutes after posting this, messages poured in, many of them focused on one aspect of her involvement on the series. If they clicked on her username, they found that she had posted in a vampire-related forum. They questioned if she really believed herself to be a vampire. She wanted to address this in one blanket post within the blended family forum.

It might be a bad move to be so openly proud of my heritage in this forum. If I am going to be a public figure, I'll have to downplay it—yet another place where I have to hide.

In a post titled, **The Truth About VickieVampire**, she wrote the following:

Hi, everyone!

Recently, I admitted that I am the Vickie who guest-stars on the popular podcast, *The Truth About the Modern Family* with Craig Watson. But there appears to be some confusion about who I am and what my real story is.

On the podcast, I've mentioned that I am a teenage girl from Austria. On a related message board, I have routinely claimed that I am a vampire with vampire abilities.

So which is it? The answer is simple: I'm a teenage girl from Austria with a history of alleged vampires in my family.

I was advised by Craig that I should not claim to

have vampire heritage on the show. This is mainly due to our credibility. He believes that claiming to have vampire ancestors on the show would not be believable, and we would not attract a good enough audience.

That's why we aren't really focused on that aspect of my life, although I talk about it openly online in other areas.

What is really happening is I have been given access to journals and other writings of my ancestors and I use those to learn more about my (apparent) vampire roots. It doesn't make me a vampire, personally, though I am involved in that community because I am curious about that sort of thing.

I love this community and the support everyone has given me and my family since we have started this podcast.

Craig's podcast is wonderful for being able to talk about my Austrian roots and the struggles of emigrating to an American family.

For those of you who are listening to the podcast, know that I really appreciate it, as does Craig. You're doing wonderful things for both of us.

Feel free to ask me anything. I'm an open book!

VickieVampire

She thought that would do the trick—downplaying her vampire heritage enough to keep people from asking further questions, while allowing her to remain online as a public figure through the podcast.

What she failed to realize was that the Circle had monitored her interactions on the message board, and by linking herself publicly to Craig Watson, they knew exactly where to find her.

She returned to scrolling through the posts on the vampire forum and another one shared by a man in Germany titled, **A Sang Journal?** caught her attention.

In the post, the man scanned several pages of a journal written in German. He was able to recognize a few bits and pieces and believed it to be written by a Sanguinarian. But he also could not read German, so he posted it for the group to see.

Vickie opened the scanned images and began to read and translate it along the way. "This isn't a journal written by a Sang," she said out loud to herself. "It's written about a Sang—by a vampire."

Our village is currently overrun with Sanguinarians, who have infiltrated every corner. It is no longer safe to walk outside alone as a vampire, knowing that our mortal enemy is waiting for us.

More concerning than their presence is their overall demeanor and attitude, both of which are unsettling.

A Sang is an empty void. A shell of a species. Sangs appear to be emotionless, expressionless, and indifferent to anything that happens around them. The empty look in their eyes drives fear into my heart, and it is impossible to concentrate or relax while in the presence of a Sang.

They also obsess over vampires. If they are in the vicinity of one, a Sang will do nothing but quietly watch every move a vampire makes. I can very rarely walk around the village without at least one of them following me. They do not appear to provoke anything, but they consistently work to make me feel uneasy.

One of the telltale signs of a Sang is their unwillingness to eat. Even when offered food by someone else, they turn the food down because they only hunger for one thing—flesh, preferably that of a human being. They thrive on their blood thirst, which is not only disturbing but also dangerous.

What angers me is the inaction of the people in our village. They know who the Sangs are. They are aware of them and yet, they do nothing about it because they fear them so much.

No one can confront the Sangs, so they walk freely.

Whenever I see a Sang with my own eyes, I feel the hatred burning in my belly.

On that last sentence, Vickie stopped reading and covered her mouth in shock. *Will is a Sang.*

Part of her didn't want to believe it, yet every piece of this description fit her interactions with the odd student.

Will obsessed over her.

He had never eaten in front of anyone.

His face was always emotionless and expressionless.

And most disturbingly, he flat-out told Vickie that they were mortal enemies. If he didn't consciously know it, he at least knew on some level that she was a vampire.

Vickie had no idea what to do. She froze in place while questions scurried around in her head with no clear answers.

What do I tell Alexis? Do I tell Alexis? Is Will here to kill me? Will he kill Alexis? How does he stay alive now? Does he kill other humans in the meantime? How did a Sang survive all this time? Are there others? Does the Circle know about him, too?

Driven by her fears and rampant thoughts, she paced in her room, unable to settle.

In a few days, she had gone from an innocent vampire

girl trying to rebuild her life to a vampire surrounded by enemies who wanted her dead.

And what was she to do about it? Would she wage war against Will? Was she supposed to sit him down and explain to him why they hated each other?

In the midst of all of these questions, her heart broke for Alexis. After all the time during which she'd waited and wished for a boy to notice her, she finally had one.

Or did she?

Was Will genuinely interested in her but also a Sang? Or was he using her to get to Vickie?

If Will is a Sang, he has many of the same powers I do. But he appears to be doing a much better job of concealing them. I wonder if he has an outlet for that energy or if he simply bottles it in like he seems to do with everything else.

Vickie sat on the edge of her bed, desperate to find any way to make sense of it all. *Will knows we're enemies. Maybe I can shift that. We could change the way that Sangs and vampires interact with each other. If the Circle knows about me, they must know about him as well. And if that's the case, we need to team up to fight them. Is that even an option? Or would Will rather deal with the Circle on his own and risk losing the fight?*

This was where her youth became a roadblock. She had no experience in dealing with Sangs directly. She didn't know how to talk to them or if there was any way to have a truce with them. It was a brand-new situation. Her parents likely knew how to deal with Sangs. But she was so young, she'd probably never learned what needed to be done.

She closed her eyes. *If there was ever a time when I could use you, dear Mutter and Vater, this would be it. I really wish you were here right now. No one else would know what I'm going through except you and only you could help me with this.*

What could she do about it? What was next? Could she confront Will at school? Or could she even be around him? There was no way to predict the next steps, and she collapsed in her bed, overcome with worry and grief.

There is no way this ends well for any of us—especially Alexis.

Before algebra class started the next day, Vickie walked up to the expressionless Will. "Meet me at the south entrance of school at four thirty today."

He looked at her and scowled. "Why?"

"We have to talk."

"That's during your cross country practice."

"I'll get out of it. And I know you'll be here anyway so instead of simply staring like you always do, be there waiting for me."

That afternoon, she told Coach Lueck she wasn't feeling well. He gave her the practice off and assured her that he was confident her conditioning wouldn't be hurt if she missed one day.

She clutched her stomach, hunched over, and moaned quietly as she walked through the halls. Once she reached a sufficient distance from the coach, she stood upright and headed to the south entrance.

Sure enough, Will waited for her, standing in front of a large blue dumpster. "I'm here. What do you want?"

The vampire pursed her lips. "You're a Sang. A biter. You're not from around here. You followed me here."

For the first time since she had ever met him, she saw him smile. "You didn't call me a vampire. You called me a Sang. That means you must be—"

"A vampire." She nodded. "That's why I feel like this around you, and that's why you hate me so much. You're right—we *are* mortal enemies."

Will folded his hands and cracked his knuckles. "Now what?"

Vickie stared at him and refused to blink. "Are you going to hurt my friend?"

He tilted his head and looked at the sky. "I haven't decided yet. It depends on how hungry I get."

Her stomach twisted and her heart pounded. As her senses heightened, her fangs grew. *It's about to go down right now, Vickie. No one else is here. Do it.*

She bared her fangs. "Stay away from Alexis."

He opened his mouth to smile and revealed his own fangs. "Try to stop me."

With all the strength she could harness, Vickie hurtled at him, lowered her shoulder, and launched him into the dumpster with such force, he dented the steel exterior.

She stepped back and he groaned in pain. As he hauled himself to his feet, he began to laugh. "You know you can't stop me, right? No vampire can stop a Sang."

Vickie balled her fists and raised them. "I won't stop trying. You won't hit a girl, will you?"

He rolled his eyes. "You're no girl. I can do whatever I want." With a demonstration of his own super-speed, Will threw a punch directly into her gut which knocked the wind out of her as she crumpled.

"Sangs always win, Vickie. Your efforts will be useless."

She focused on the idea that he was the heavy punching bag Craig had set up for her and launched a thundering crossover punch to his jaw. He spun a few times before he sprawled on the pavement.

Will laughed, his jaw hanging open. She had dislocated it, but he placed his hand on his jaw, pushed on it, and it snapped back into place. "I have many of the same abilities you do, Vickie. There's only one way to get rid of me, and I doubt you can pull it off." He dragged his thumb symbolically across his throat.

Vickie hissed with rage, tackled him, and sank her fangs into the side of his neck. He growled in pain and kicked her off.

She flipped onto her back, but Will hung onto her arm and bit her flesh. Her moan was instinctual, but she gritted her teeth to stifle the sound as much as she could. She punched him in the side of the head, which loosened his grip so she could scramble free of him.

They sat on the ground and stared at one another. Blood flowed from the side of Will's neck and from her forearm. The combatants each took a moment to force their wounds to close before they tensed and gathered their strength for another bout.

Footsteps pounded the pavement in a rapid approach.

Will shook his head and smiled. "Better luck next time." He engaged his super-speed and vanished in the moment when she took a breath to respond.

The vampire ducked hastily behind the dumpster so no

one would see the blood on her arm. *I don't want anyone to ask questions. If I wait here for the coast to be clear, I can get inside and wash up.*

The boys' cross country team crossed the parking lot and jogged past her. When they were a safe distance away, she emerged from behind the dumpster to head inside.

Vickie paused as she ran her fingers along the massive dent their altercation had left on the huge trashcan. *This will only get worse.*

CHAPTER THIRTY

Hannes stepped off the elevator and looked out of the windows directly in front of him. It was another gray day. Little activity took place outside the hotel. The air was crisp, and most people had chosen to stay inside.

He walked down the hall and unlocked his room with the keycard. When the light on the handle turned green, he pushed down on the lever, walked into the room, and closed the door behind him.

"That's everything," he announced. "We made it."

"Excellent." Gabriel stood from the couch to retrieve a long, padded black bag. He hoisted it onto the bed in the second room of the two-bedroom suite and unzipped it. Carefully, he opened the cover to reveal the long, heavy sword of the Circle. "Perfectly intact. Very good."

"Will we bring it with us, sir?" Noah asked as he walked into the room behind him.

The leader shook his head. "Not this time. We want to move quickly, but we do not need to be in a rush. If we hurry unnecessarily, we make mistakes. We're here, and

243

that's all that matters right now. Let's first assess the situation, then make our plans."

Hannes nodded and used his phone to order an Uber. "We have ten minutes, so we should get ready and head downstairs."

He slipped a pair of gloves in his coat pocket for good measure. The men shrugged into thick jackets and winter hats. They left the room and rode the elevator down to the main floor. By the time they reached the front entrance, their driver was waiting for them.

The three rode silently through the city. An airplane roared overhead and Hannes almost pressed his face up against the car window to watch it ascend. *I wish I was on that plane instead of here. I really don't look forward to any of this.*

After about half an hour of driving, they stopped near a public park. Noah thanked the driver and they all exited in silence.

Hannes shivered. "It's colder here than it was at the airport."

Noah zipped his coat higher to cover his neck. "I can't believe so many people would be out here on a day like this."

"All right now, let's all act naturally," Gabriel ordered. "We are here as fans. Let's find out where we need to go."

"I'll find a map." Hannes jogged over to a long table manned by several volunteers, accepted a packet with *WISCONSIN STATE QUALIFYING MEET* emblazoned across the top, and returned to the group. "This is good," he said as he flipped it open. "We have a map along with a listing of all the names."

The leader snatched it from his hands and turned the pages until he saw the team rosters. "There." He pointed to the listing for Clear Lake High School. The fifth name was Vickie Hewitt. "She will be the fifth runner for that team."

Hannes and Noah enjoyed the excitement that spilled from the event. People were everywhere, and there was a vital energy in the air.

"I can see the girls already at the starting line," he told them. "That means we need to find a place where we will be able to identify her clearly."

The three of them followed the map to an obscure spot in the woods, about halfway through the course. As they settled in to wait, the starter's pistol fired.

"What was that?" Noah asked, wide-eyed.

"It's only the start of the race," Hannes replied. "Take it easy."

"Blend in, gentlemen. We are fans here." Gabriel put his hands in his pockets, his expression calm as he waited for the runners.

As the first few barreled down the path, he clapped with the appearance of enthusiasm to cheer them on. The others followed suit. Several Clear Lake High School runners passed them.

"I counted three. That means one more and the next will be her."

A few minutes later, the fourth runner for Clear Lake ran past. Finally, Vickie appeared, holding her role as the fifth man for their team.

She had settled into a good pace, but as she approached the wooded area, she began to slow. Her stomach hurt worse than it ever had. *Ow. Something bad is happening. Here. Right now. Something very, very bad.*

The pain was almost crippling as she ran past the three men. They stared intently at her. She tried to shake it off and keep running and struggled to return her focus to the race. As she put a little distance between herself and them, her stomach began to relax.

Still, the sense of danger had been so strong, she had almost stopped the race.

"That was her." Gabriel nodded. "That was the last vampire girl. We have found her. And now, we can move to the next phase—to formulate a plan to exterminate her."

Vickie finished the race and helped to put her team in a position to qualify for the state cross country meet held in Oconomowoc, Wisconsin, in two weeks. The girls cheered, high-fived, and hugged.

She joined the celebrations, but in the back of her mind, she reeled with the implications of what she had experienced. *I felt a strange presence on this course today. The Circle felt closer than it ever has, for some reason.*

Coach Lueck congratulated them on a fine race. "It was exactly what we needed to get to State as a team. I'm very proud of you girls, and I can't wait to see if you can finish the season with the state championship."

After his little pep talk, he noticed that Vickie's mind was on other things. He walked over to her. "Is everything okay?"

"Yeah. Yeah, but I'm a little distracted right now." She shook her head as if she tried to shake the cobwebs out.

"You can let yourself get distracted for the rest of the day if you want. You did fantastic work out there. Vickie, you've done such a great job as our fifth man this season. I'm glad you were able to work your way up onto the Varsity squad. How do you feel about our chances at State?"

"You know better than I do, Coach," she said. "I'll simply go out there and do my best."

"Hey, that's all I can ask of you." He slapped her on the back. "I have to watch the boys' race. Way to go today." He jogged away to find a suitable viewing place on the course.

The vampire wanted to cheer the boys on, especially Eric. But she had felt so sick from whatever it was that had affected her so intensely while she ran that she sat on a picnic table for a few minutes and simply tried to rest and reset her mind.

First Will, now this. It seems like being a vampire is following me around wherever I go. Even when I try to live a normal life, it follows.

This realization frustrated her and also brought a slight sense of despondency. All she wanted was a normal life, but the longer she stayed there, the less normal everything became.

At the end of the meet, the boys did not qualify for the state championship race. Vickie was there to console Eric afterward, who was heartbroken.

"We worked so hard. I thought we had it this year," he said dejectedly.

"You'll get there next year," she assured him. He thanked her and made sure she knew that he would be at the state meet to cheer her on with everything he had. She smiled and kissed him.

Off in the distance, Noah turned to his accomplices. "She kissed that boy. He must be a boyfriend of some kind."

"That could be a weakness we can exploit." Gabriel rubbed his hands together to keep them warm. "It's certainly something we need to pay attention to. We need to know everything about this girl's life—who she spends time with, what her family looks like, what her days look like, everything."

"It feels like a fact-finding mission, sir." Hannes tried to hide his disappointment, which was also tinged with a vague sense of relief.

"I'm only talking about the first phase of our plan." The leader scowled at him. "We need to learn before we can act. This way, we will know her every move. That will make the job even easier."

Back at the picnic table, Vickie clutched her stomach.

"Are you hungry or something? I have snacks."

"No thanks. I'm only having some health issues."

Eric stiffened. "Seriously?"

"Yeah, but don't act like it's serious. It's not. Only some mild discomfort, that's all. I'll be fine."

Everyone returned to the bus, cheering for the girls and their state qualification. The vehicle drove off and the three men in the woods watched it turn left, and they assumed they could find the high school from there.

Their expectations weren't unfounded. Fifteen minutes after leaving the meet, the Circle members lingered across the street from the high school and the track and football field.

"When do we get to use the sword?" Noah asked.

"We will use the sword when the right opportunity

presents itself," Gabriel said. "I have full confidence that, provided we are in this for the long haul, we will be able to exact revenge on the vampire race and finally end this forever."

"And the other species we detected?" Hannes asked.

"One thing at a time. We found the girl. The last vampire is in our sights. This is good. If there really is another, we will have to wait and find out. But our priority right now, above all else, is to kill the girl with that sword, exactly like our forefathers would have wanted us to do. It's time to purge this world from evil once again."

The Circle is now in the U.S. and coming for Vicki. Can she protect her family and herself from them? Find out in THE GIRL IN PLAIN SIGHT

**Find the compass, save the world or
save herself?**

Dating is harder for Maggie Parker than running down a
felon. Now add in magic.

Did she just see a compass fly?

Can she learn how to use the magic of bubbles to chart
a new course in time? It's a lot harder than it sounds.

Join her on her quest to rescue passengers on an
ancient ship – a big blue marble called Earth – and save
herself.

<u>**AVAILABLE ON AMAZON AND IN KINDLE
UNLIMITED!**</u>

Years ago, I used to think that a journey of change or growth was largely taken alone. Sure, I asked for help, read books, went to seminars, there were a few sweat lodges and vision quests in there too. But in the end, I was on a solitary road trip. Everything I read, saw or heard encouraged that idea. We are born alone, we die alone, we mingle for a while at intermittent times while we're here.

I've ditched that idea. I'd rather change in a cooperative and go wide with it. Why not? Studies of all kinds of animals – both prey and predator – including human beings, has shown that it's in our DNA to work as a group with a majority consensus. When we compete against each other, we're fighting our evolution. When we build things together, we're in the flow.

It's a messier tack to take. Humans rarely put things back where they found it. They say things that are awkward. They're messy and celebrate the holidays differently than you do, and they carry around fears and small bits of anger that can bubble up without notice.

I'm okay with all of that.

They're also courageous, creative, inventive, and best of all – carry an innate belief that things can change for the better. It's our natural reset button. Sure, for some of us that button has gotten jammed, or even broken, but that's not a permanent condition. Remove the old beliefs that were based on bad info, fix the reset button. It's possible for anyone reading this – you'll have to trust me on that.

To that end, let's create a tribe. In fact, I've already started. The Peabrain Society, which started as an offshoot of The Peabrain Adventures series, is growing into something bigger. With the help of my team, and Joe Solari, we're creating a place where we can bring our dreams – big and small – and get on that journey today – together. There will be two rules in this place (same two there already are) – no naming and shaming and no self-promotion. Other than that, we're gonna figure out a few things and look toward the solution – one step, one day at a time.

I have a saying – Never Ask Somebody to Do Something You Aren't Willing to Do Yourself. To that end, my two biggest dreams right now are to lose weight so all the clothes in my closet that currently mock me – fit again. And then to date with conviction (in other words – can't give up after a few bad ones). I've been taking pictures of me at the start and I'm documenting my progress in the Facebook Group and on Instagram – and I'm going to do it with all of you – everyone who cares to can join me with their thing they want to do.

Tools to help you get out of your way, get inspired, be kinder to yourself, let go and fix that button – will be coming as well, plus a lot more. Stay tuned – and by the way – already down just about one size. Progress. More adventures to follow.

THANK YOU for not only reading this story but these *Author Notes* as well.

(I think I've been good with always opening with "thank you." If not, I need to edit the other *Author Notes*!)

RANDOM (*sometimes*) THOUGHTS?

What would you do if scientists from another country confirmed there was evidence of aliens?

Would you fist-pump the air and say "YES!" or would the fact it was another country cause you to pause?

The reason I ask is I was reading an article about a possible alien structure orbiting a (very far away) star. The area has been questioned for many years, and so far, all of the obvious reasons for the abnormality seen so far can't be true.

Except one (according to the scientist). The one that might be true has to do with a lot of comets somehow being pulled together. The scientist goes on to explain it is incredibly unlikely comets pulled together without being swallowed by the sun etc.

I'm just curious why the statements about assuming it can't be aliens are in these statements?

I mean, if you were on another planet and you found Earth, would it be so odd that this planet had life and they "could be aliens?"

Seriously?

If you are religious (specifically Christian), the Bible already talks about aliens.

If you are not religious, then what are the freaking odds that the universe is so large, with so many planets, and life hasn't occurred somewhere else?

Personally, I think the attitude about potential life in other areas of the galaxy not happening is sticking a proverbial head in the sand.

Then again, I'm a science-fiction and fantasy author.

Of course, I want aliens to exist.

Just like I want (nice) Vampires to exist. Until we can prove it, I'll have to keep making up vampire stories.

AROUND THE WORLD IN 80 DAYS

One of the interesting (at least to me) aspects of my life is the ability to work from anywhere and at any time. In the future, I hope to re-read my own *Author Notes* and remember my life as a diary entry.

Los Angeles, California USA

I'm sitting here in the LAX airport (Terminal 5 - Rock and Brews) enjoying a little peace (well, that's subjective) and quiet (totally a lie - the music is jamming) writing up my *Author Notes* for book four million three hundred and thirty thousand…and five.

(Also a complete fabrication of the most audacious kind.)

On the TV are two baseball games (I've no idea). Also, Great White's *Rock Me* (the video) is playing, and I'm reliving some scenes of my early twenties.

Damn, good times!

I'm fifty-two years old and having a blast. Unfortunately, the whole weight thing is absolutely a problem for me now as well. All of the sitting on me back-end-bus and eating delicious food (like I was still in my twenties) is not sitting well.

Sorry, I'm having a bout of 'don't give a @#@#' about the weight. MORE COKE PLEASE!

I'm well aware that (for me) the weight can come off if I'll just pay more attention to the food (quantity and type) and do some exercise.

The challenge is as I've gotten older, I want to do less physical activity, more hibernation (often in little snippets like from the desk, to the couch, to the bed, and start all over again the next day.)

OH OH! *Down Under* from MEN AT WORK is playing on the TV. (I don't think I've ever seen the video.)

It's a silly song, but it has plastered a smile on my face.

FAN PRICING

$0.99 Saturdays (new LMBPN stuff) and $0.99 Wednesday (both LMBPN books and friends of LMBPN books.) Get great stuff from us and others at tantalizing prices.

Go ahead. I bet you can't read just one.

Sign up here: http://lmbpn.com/email/.

HOW TO MARKET FOR BOOKS YOU LOVE

Review them so others have your thoughts, and tell friends and the dogs of your enemies (because who wants to talk to enemies?)... *Enough said ;-)*

Ad Aeternitatem,

Michael Anderle

JOIN THE ORICERAN UNIVERSE FAN GROUP ON FACEBOOK!

www.ingramcontent.com/pod-product-compliance
Lightning Source LLC
Chambersburg PA
CBHW050238110726
47898CB00007B/2188